The
Letter
Bearer

The
Letter
Bearer

ROBERT ALLISON

GRANTA

Granta Publications, 12 Addison Avenue, London W11 4QR

First published in Great Britain by Granta Books, 2014

Copyright © Robert Allison, 2014

A CIP catalogue record for this book is available
from the British Library.

1 3 5 7 9 10 8 6 4 2

ISBN 978 1 84708 823 9 (hardback)
ISBN 978 1 84708 824 6 (trade paperback)

Typeset by M Rules

Printed and bound by CPI Group (UK) Ltd, Croydon, CR0 4YY

To my parents

NORTH AFRICA

1942

One

1

He wakes in the desert, surprised to hear the anthem for his funeral. 'Bye Bye Blackbird' – Gene Austin, Victor Orthophonic Recording – its refrain rising above the descant of flies.

On his back, he sees himself foreshortened, his limbs defined by a riot of wings. His greatcoat spread at his sides, its weave shot through, the tracery to some fierce onslaught. Towering from the crimp of his khaki drill shirt is a metal rib, brilliant with sunglare. Quite painless, unless he moves.

Oh, what a hard luck story.

Gm-C⁷-F-Dm

Other melodies come to him. 'In the Mood' – The Glenn Miller Orchestra, 'There's a New Day Coming' – Harry Roy and His Orchestra. The Adagio to Bruckner's Eighth: serene, ecstatic. In the next life, he thinks, I shall be a musician, composing a rag to misadventure. The sand humming, his fingers laying the beat, inselbergs and yardangs in song. He purses his lips to whistle.

A mistake. The spittle from his coughing draws the flies. They will press into the breach, laying eggs in his throat. His sun-blackened cadaver expanding and contracting, sitting at breakfast, reclining at supper. The puppetry of maggots: he has seen it. Dying will be a dirge.

Heat boils him back to the moment. The shadows of rock pylons newly canted, lazy clock hands across the desert floor. No perpendiculars, only inclinations, a parchment of obliques. His forehead is soused in sweat, likewise the hollow of his throat, the cave of skin below his breastbone. The membrane over his lips has lifted away.

He turns his head, disturbing the flies. Through the tinted celluloid of his goggles an acreage of orange scree billows into tall hummocks, sandstone reefs scooped by the currents. In the next life, he thinks, I shall be an artist, making a *guazzo* of this bare ocean.

There is even a wreck, lying some three yards behind him, hanging from a vine of black smoke. A motorcycle collapsed onto its haunches, its wheels crumpled like bottle caps. He has no memory of it.

Pain arcs through him, causing him to grasp at the sand, and for an instant he sees the picture of himself in the embedded shard. His last, strange portrait before he is to be reduced, dispersed into the sand.

The pain recedes, and he closes his eyes to imagine himself quitting his own body, spiralling downward, becoming unplottable. How far to the centre of the earth? How far to the underworld? His name understood there as ———, an Elysian murmur, a sonance unknowable to the living. Only the dry kernel of him left to mark the ground above.

A man with dark moons for eyes crouches over him. Black lenses stitched into a wrap of hide. His peaked cap displaying the insignia of a pale blue eagle over tricolour cockade.

𝕯𝖊𝖚𝖙𝖘𝖈𝖍𝖊𝖘 𝕬𝖋𝖗𝖎𝖐𝖆𝖐𝖔𝖗𝖕𝖘

'Tommy? Tommy, can you hear me? Nice motorcycle, Tommy. Matchless Three-fifty cc. Overhead valve. Teledraulic fork. Good for the bumps.' He hoists the sand goggles onto his forehead. 'I know British motorcycles. Norton side valve. Velocette. BSA. I rode an Empire Star with sidecar. Very reliable, almost as good as German. But our Zündapp has *Sperrdifferential*. *Hydraulische* brakes. It's the future. I said to my older brother to have my BSA but he bought a Benelli instead. Can you believe this? A Benelli. I said to him, don't buy this Italian shit. They make nothing to last. Just like the mine you rode over. Rusted detonator wires, you see. The smallest touch and boom! *Italienischer Schrott*. Your Matchless is kaput, Tommy. Are you thirsty?'

Yes. Where did you come from? I blinked and you were here.

'It's okay, Tommy. Don't try to talk.' He uncaps a felted canteen and brings the nozzle to the wounded man's mouth. 'So you were a rider, a postman. I looked in your bag. Letters home. That's a nice thing, Tommy. A great thing for your friends.' The flask smells of cordite and gun oil, the water as warm as saliva. 'Not so smart to ride without a helmet, Tommy. Even here. I'm going to take off your goggles, okay?'

Okay.

'Can you see? You have blood in your eyes.'

Yes. Are you my confessor?

'Tommy, there's shrapnel between your ribs. I shouldn't pull it out. There'll be infection soon. Your lungs may be damaged. Have you had morphine?'

No.

'*Warum beschäftigst du dich noch mit ihm? Lass ihn einfach in Ruhe!*' The DAK man's comrade is sitting in the sidecar of a sand-painted combo two dozen yards distant. '*Das ist Zeitverschwendung.*' It's pointless, he's finished!

'If I had morphine I would give it to you, Tommy. One moment.'

Yes, okay. I'll wait.

The DAK man walks over to his fellow in the sidecar and speaks with him. He returns to unholster a pistol.

'Tommy. There's nobody near. Nobody coming. It doesn't look good for you.' He flicks off the safety, slides back the toggle. 'I want to do what's best for you. If you understand, just nod.'

Certainly. Can you hear my funeral anthem?

The DAK man aims at the rider's forehead. *Gott mit uns, Tommy.*

Click.

Click 2. *Scheisse.*

Click 3. *Arschloch.*

The DAK man frowns at the weapon. Sand in the firing mechanism? A dud round? Mistress Fortuna?

Italienisch? the rider thinks to enquire.

The DAK man looks to his compatriot then shakes his head and holsters the pistol. 'What's your name, Tommy?'

————.

He crouches and inspects the rider's ID tags, an olive-drab octagon, a brick-red disc.

'Tommy, can I take these? *Als Talismane. Glücksbringer.*'

Yes, take them. I don't need them any more.

'*Seine Uhr!*' The fellow in the sidecar again.

The DAK man undoes the rider's wristwatch. 'I'm not stealing this from you. After the war I'll find you again. I'll give it back.' He searches the pockets of the rider's greatcoat and pulls out a small brown pay book. He flips the pages. 'You see? Now I can find you. Maybe then we can be friends.' He unbuttons a pocket on his field blouse and withdraws a crumpled packet. '*Möchten Sie eine Zigarette?* Victory V?'

Victory V = pee. I think I might wet myself. Don't you have Woodbines? Players Medium?

The DAK man lights a cigarette and places it between the

rider's lips. The rider coughs and blows a bubble of blood, the cigarette toppling onto his chin. The DAK man plucks it clear and wedges it between the rider's fingers. 'So now I have to go, Tommy.'

No, don't go. Stay.

'Better for your eyes to wear the goggles.'

But I don't want you to go.

The DAK man rises and walks back to his comrade in the side-car. He kick-starts the motorcycle and gestures down towards it. 'BMW. Always a good starter. Not like a shit Benelli.' He twists the throttle, the combo throwing up a spume of dust as it motors away. His companion gazing back, expressionless, as the heat gathers them up.

The cigarette burns down to the rider's fingers, causing him to snatch his hand away. Victory V = …

He doesn't fight the sensation this time, allowing his bladder to empty. That precious physic which cools Vickers gun barrels, refills radiators. That when trodden upon toughens the soles of the feet. In the desert, one wastes nothing. He turns his head to see the postbag lying beside the broken motorcycle, ransacked and close to empty.

I was a rider, a postman. A great thing.

At night the crackle of dunes gives way to a cantata of sighs. The cold now entering via the channel of steel in his breast, vitrifying the bones, congealing the blood. His heart is beating quicker, his breaths shorter, the muscles of his arms and legs stiffening. The end, he supposes, must be near.

He pulls off his goggles, the moon an exit wound in the blackness. He recognises the Dog Star, the constellation of the Hunter. He remembers the rotating charts from *The Observer's Planisphere of Air Navigation Stars* (Francis Chichester). Key to the Indestructibles.

A scuttle between the rocks alarms him, those creatures who secrete themselves by day now busy. Something skitters over his hand, making him start, and he tries uselessly to shift position, his legs heavy and inert. This wretched sentence!

He closes his eyes, trying again for detachment. But there is no peace in the dark, images of a furious conflagration insisting upon him. The roiling carcass of a tank, its tracks slipped from its wheels, the steel of its hull phosphor-bright, oil smoke vented in magic-lantern staccato. He runs towards it but too late, each step a fatal interval. A man emerges hauling the drape of his skin behind him, two others fused into a single trunk as they heave themselves up, both blanketed in fire.

He trembles at the sudden compression of gravel, the slide of grit. Some sly predator, bearing upon him unseen! He waves an arm, crying out with the effort of it, a brawl of pale robes already dazzling the corner of his eye. A white *keffiyeh*. Then quick black eyes.

The vagabonds whisper to one another in a mysterious tongue while they ransack his clothes, his pockets, imparting in their closeness a train of balms: oiled goatskin, sumac, za'atar, tincture of frankincense. They take from him a small magnifying glass, an

ID card, a pocketknife, a silk map from the waistband of his tunic, the buttons from his pockets. They find an envelope in his shirt pocket and toss it aside, then turn him over to complete their ransack, the sensation dizzying to him. They rummage his postbag, then strip the Matchless of its battery and its leather seat before stealing away, pale *gallabiyas* tapering into the dark. If he had the fluids for it he would weep. The nausea is worse, the pain worse, the body's poisons welling. He looks again to the motor-cycle, seeing in that moment the tale of it. The hot breeze as he had put his head down into the wind, the sting of dust, the huffing of Teledraulic forks over rises and gullies. The shock as he had been snatched up by a ferocious bloom of air, the Matchless careering end over end. His first thought afterwards: that he had bitten his tongue.

He uses his elbows and heels to draw himself towards the wreck. He gathers the postbag to him and pushes any loose letters back inside. Then pulls the bag beneath his head as a pillow. This is where I will stay, he thinks. With all these names.

2

Can you hear?

How is the pain now?

Are you dizzy?

A finger is brought close to his face, drawn to the right, then left, up, down. An infant's learning game.

How many fingers now?

What do you see?

A half-lit world. The moon over ironstone, Cassiopeia rising. What can he see? Three fingers. Then four. Then two. (Is it two?) Nothing of purpose.

Are you thirsty?

Yes.

They put a mug to his lips, and mop his brow as he coughs.

*

They had come for him in the dark. Given him water and lifted him onto a stretcher then ferried him to an ambulance. Not an ambulance proper but a lightweight truck daubed with a red cross, his stretcher wedged between jerrycans on its hardwood bed. They had driven without headlights while he had watched the stars leap, his head lolling in the fetors of gasoline, grease and rubber. One of his rescuers had smoked a cigarette, its tip shrouded with a holed tin to douse the glow, and he had turned around every now and then to call through the canvas. Not far now, just hold on.

They had brought him to an encampment without lamp or fire-light, a modest leaguer comprising several small tents and a parked Quad tractor, a squat, blockish vehicle designed to haul twenty-five-pounder guns. He had been lifted from the truck and taken into one of the tents, several sombre-faced spectators following. They had laid him on an iron-framed bunk, where they had cut the urinous and sweat-lathered clothes from him while he had spun helices about himself, his bearings still aligned to a yawing axle. Soon have you shipshape, one of them had said. Got to you just in the nick.

'Sorry about the piss,' he'd mumbled.

One of his benefactors had sat on a locker by his bedside. 'Can you tell us your name?' A chorister's voice, pitched in the higher registers.

He would have replied with an aria if he'd had the air. Instead he had shaken his head. 'The Germans took it.'

How many?/From what direction?/Just one vehicle?/Are you certain?

'No. I'm not certain.'

They had anointed his skin with iodine, then burst the thin flesh of his hip to introduce that grand elixir of calm. He had drawn it into his veins and swum in the warmth of it, absolved. The fellow with the cigarette patting his shoulder as he had risen to leave, saying, 'We brought your letters.' As though they were the very sum and essence of him.

There is a stain on the side of the tent which fascinates him now, a Rorschachian smear given definition by the light of early morning. He is blind to its colour because all he sees is red. It might be grease. It might be blood. A sudarium wrought in the sanguine and phlegmatic humours. A man might discover himself this way, by printing one's face in three dimensions and scouting its uncharted defiles. Journeys of the cheekbone and brow, a cartography of fascia and bone.

But such notions can no longer distract him from himself, the discomfort from bruised muscles and torn skin pushing through narcoma, his hearing chambered and dull except for an insistent, high-pitched tone. In the roof of his mouth his tongue finds new pits and hollows, the palate bloodily re-engineered. The shard of metal has gone from his chest, replaced by a square pad of lint, but beneath it he can still feel the ridge of skin. And now the flies are returning. At first one by one and then in groups, buzzing and crawling through the loose flap of tent, settling on the offcuts of bandages and kidney bowls of carbolic. Their assault soon mounting to a full-fledged invasion, forcing him to shrink beneath his woollen blanket. And still their tiny heads and forelegs push inside.

He is close to tears. Why is there no more morphine? The effort of holding up the blanket makes him wheeze. He wants to cry out, but he has no breath for it. *How can they leave me like this?*

It seems an age before a medical orderly appears to calm him and brush away his tormentors, then to offer a mug of tea as if nothing at all has happened. There's a biscuit with marmalade, if he fancies. How is his breathing now?

A trial. May I have more morphine?

When the orderly leans over to administer the injection, the rider notices that the man's eyelids are swollen and discoloured as though by fire, the flesh of his brow similarly melted then sealed. And he is filled with wonder at this patient minister, whom he decides must be the archdeacon of opiates.

When he wakes again, he is called upon by the fellow who had questioned him at his bedside and who now gives his name as Brinkhurst, Ranulph.

'Can't offer you much in the way of scoff, I'm afraid. Just the usual Fray Bentos, some tinned sausage meat. Perhaps we can rustle you up a stew, something easy to swallow. Cup of cha, how would that be?'

Brinkhurst, he thinks, is an officer, but without the insignia to declare it. Slight in build but bearing the bale of jurisdiction, the type to sit with another and assume a hierarchy. Were it not for his sandblasted face, one might think him a country gentleman, a patrician whose world view might be served up in a shot glass. Yet he introduces himself without title. Soldiery as a workers' collective, perhaps.

He says he will try to eat, and Brinkhurst seems gratified. Before leaving he pegs back the tent flaps to allow a wider view of the leaguer, and it takes a minute for the rider's eyes to adjust to the glare. What had seemed in the darkness a modest arrangement appears in daylight more impoverished still, a schoolboy's conceit in sticks and rags, a few canvas dens punctuating the flatness of a natural depression, the settlement's boundary scored by slit trenches. The truck he was brought in on is parked alongside the Quad, each draped with scrim. Behind them is a small corral fenced with barbed wire in which two chickens bob and peck. And then a wide ditch overfilled with automotive debris and weeping oilcans. At the furthest reach of the camp there is a small cairn of stones, its crucifix fashioned from the helves of entrenching tools.

Brinkhurst reappears carrying a mess tin of bully stew and a mug of cocoa, both covered with lids. 'Courtesy of the cookhouse,' he says. The rider heaves himself upright on his mattress, mustering himself with a steady inhalation. He sets the tin on his lap and sifts the stew with a spoon, leaving one hand free to bat at flies. 'Cookhouse' is a flattery. He can see it through the opened tent, a crude fabrication of tin sheet and sandbags, only its apex rising above the surface, its greater measure lodged in the cooler earth. Beside it is a pyramid of stone-filled cans serving as a rudimentary water filter, and then a shallower dugout lined with corrugated sheeting and half-filled with sand. A rectangular 'flimsy' petrol can with a hose attached sits over the pit, a makeshift tap fitted to control the flow of fuel. An ingenuity that here verges on the Hellenistic.

'Coming back to you yet? Anything?' It's implicit in Brinkhurst's tone. What soldier could forget his station?

The rider shakes his head, tentative in his swallowing.

'Your uniform had no markings of rank, no colours.'

But there's nothing for the rider to add, leaving Brinkhurst somewhat chagrined. 'So I suppose you've no idea of the score?'

The rider notices that his interrogator has the habit of repeatedly drawing his index finger from his lip to his ear and palpating the jaw muscle. The motion of unzipping himself, pulling back the officer carapace to reveal the commoner beneath.

'Where are we?'

Brinkhurst dips his forefinger in a dish of carbolic then rubs onto the tent's canvas the contour of a long coastline, topped by the reclined head of a giant. He points out two locations close to one another. 'Derna and Tobruk.' He drags his finger further down the map. 'El Adem.' He trails his fingertip downward until it is dry. 'And here's the spot. Or thereabouts.'

The rider nods, impressed that they have moved into uncharted country.

'It's the last day of May,' adds Brinkhurst. 'In case you were wondering. You've been out nearly two days.'

The rider lifts another spoonful of stew. 'How did you find me?'

'Plain luck. Swann over there was on a recce when he spotted smoke.' He gestures towards a bare-chested fellow inspecting the truck's tyres, the tattoo of a cobra winding up his right arm onto his shoulder. 'We guessed it would be a mine. Bloody Ities dropped a truckload of them here when they were trying to wipe out the locals. Have to mind how you go.'

The rider watches Swann as he squats to peer beneath the truck. The perfect antipode of his name, showing nothing of the elegant, the flexuous. He moves with a determined weight, giving nothing to the sand.

'The letters you had,' says Brinkhurst. 'They're all from the same battalion. Third Tank Regiment.'

Swann realises he is being studied and zones in on the rider's gaze, holding it briefly before dismissing him.

Brinkhurst is undeterred. 'Were you a DR for battalion HQ? With Signals, perhaps? Postal Unit?'

The rider gags on a mouthful of stew, the coordination of breathing and eating suddenly lost to him.

'It's all right, don't worry.' Brinkhurst lifts away the mess tin and spoon. 'I'll have Mawdsley look in on you.'

The rider mops spittle from his chin and wipes his eyes. He examines his chest dressing for a widening stain, the pain worse again. When he looks up, Swann is stooping at the tent's entrance, shirt in his hand.

'I'm takin' her out,' he says, displaying at this range a youngster's face, unlined, the broad and full cheeks implying a geniality. The rider recognises his Scottish accent from the truck and is beset by a sudden envy, that a man can become so unmistakable by his phonology. If his own voice carries such clues of geography then they are quite inaudible to him.

Brinkhurst frowns. 'I thought we'd agreed.' (The hint of West Country, a battened rusticity?)

'I agreed to tell you is all.' Swann pulls on his shirt, its sleeve displaying the emblem of a stag's head above the single chevron of a lance corporal. He saunters back to the truck and loads it with several jerrycans, each marked with a white cross. He fires up the engine to a steady growl and steers the truck from the lea-guer, its suspension squeaking as the vehicle wallows over uneven ground.

And all is at once clear. The lack of a command structure, the putting aside of rank. This is not some specialist unit, or even the dogged remnants of one, but rather a corpus of the disaffected. These men have made the desert their bolt-hole.

Brinkhurst registers the alarm of comprehension. 'We do things our own way here. We do what works best. You'll see for yourself.' He rises. 'You should probably rest for a bit.'

A flush of panic overcomes the rider. There will be no hos-pital, no specialists, no surgeons. His body is to subsist in its corrupted state. *Do they have enough morphine?* 'I need to see a doctor. I have more pain. Just here, going through to my back.'

'Mawdsley will set you straight. I'll have him come right away.'

Brinkhurst makes his exit. Let him know, he adds, if there's any recall of fact or detail. It could be critical.

The rider leans back, enveloped for a time in his own tides, the soundscape of an underwater swimmer. He looks on as the wind picks up dust outside the tent, others in the camp now and then passing by, offering a cursory acknowledgement or none at all. A listless theatre. Perhaps in this ruined state he will live out the last of his time, inanimate, a pedlar of gazes.

But such diversions dull with the light, leaving only the imaginary to captivate, a fleeting escape to be made in the conjuring of a cityscape, of minarets ranked against a lowering sky. And in the foreground, a grand basilica drawn out from the buttresses of the encircling basalt, its ramparts swelling to a vast and pearlescent rotunda. A great desert shrine, secret to all but the wounded and confused. If he narrows his eyes he can see within it a maze of archways leading to a chimney of floodlit space. And then a figure emerging from the immensity of light. Legs adrift, bird head of Ra. His form becoming gradually human as he approaches the rider's tent, his long-limbed frame folding as he bows to enter. When he stands tall again and removes his peaked cap, he shows a polite smile. Though there's no distracting from that brow of seared flesh.

Terrell Mawdsley, he says. Come to answer a summons.

A Litany

'You're going to feel rather sore, I'm afraid. There's quite a bit of heavy bruising. Some laceration. Nothing broken except a cheekbone. We took a two-inch piece of shrapnel from between your ribs. The stitches will feel tight. Try to avoid sudden exertion, stretches. That kind of thing.

'I think both of your eardrums are perforated. It's difficult to tell with the inflammation. The sulphonamide tablets will help prevent infection. The dizziness and nausea are probably vertigo. That should go.

'As for your eyes, I don't know what to tell you. You say everything is red. It sounds like the retinas might be damaged. Perhaps some part of the brain. I'm not an optician.

'This confusion you're experiencing. The amnesia, the disorientation. It's to be expected. An explosive force tearing through your head. Some memories might have gone completely. Blown away, so to speak. You might find yourself emotional, angry. That would be normal.

'The worst problem is your lungs. You need to understand this. It's the pressure of the air moving through your body, the vacuum when it draws back again. It ruptures the tiny structures of the lung wall, causing unstable pressures, oedema, air emboli. The lungs can't heal. A hospital wouldn't help. I'm sorry. I think you should know.

'It's hard to predict from here. No one can say. I once saw a man in your condition go on for several weeks. Luck plays a part, one's general vitality. We should be able to make you comfortable.

'This new pain you report, it sounds like constipation. Shock would do that. The morphine would have made it worse. We should give you a laxative. Outside would be best. The flies, and all. As soon as you feel able.

'I'll leave this pen and paper. You might want to write down anything you remember. Your name, if it comes to you. Your religion.

'I'm sorry I can't do more. I'll look in on you later. Sleep would be best now. As long as you can. It won't help to be awake.'

3

In the morning Mawdsley comes to see him again, bringing a cup of sterile-tasting tea and some biscuits with marmalade. He listens to the rider's breathing. 'How did you sleep?'

'The gut cramps are worse.'

Mawdsley inspects his arm. 'You've been bitten. Let me see.' He lifts the edge of the blanket, revealing several red bumps on the rider's legs. 'Sand lice. We usually debug the place every few days. They crawl out of nowhere. Anyway, your bowels. We shouldn't wait.'

He gives the rider a No. 9 pill, guaranteed to do the trick of flushing him, and enlists a recalcitrant Swann to help him outside. It has the flavour of an execution, the convicted man naked except for his blanket, brittle from the punishments already inflicted. The lance corporal guides him to some stowage boxes and helps him sit. 'Don't do it here,' he says. 'Not near the burner. Shout when you're ready.'

The rider pulls his blanket tighter.

Swann joins Mawdsley in dragging everything from the rider's tent: metal bed frame, mattress, lockers, bins, blankets, clothing. They dismantle the frame and beat the pieces with a spade to dislodge the insects inside, stamping them underfoot before repeating the procedure for the lockers and bins. They shake the materials and fabrics and lay them out on the ground for Swann to soak in paraffin, the rider shading his eyes to watch. Mawdsley collects a blowlamp and begins setting light to any metal or hardwood items, paying particular attention to any corners or recesses. A man perfectly at ease, notes the rider, with the element of his ruin.

Swann calls to the rider, asking if he is ready to unload his bowels, then glares when he shakes his head. Any respectable soldier of course being able to shit on command.

The rider looks away from him to survey the outlying terrain, the camp's flat basin encircled by a towering ring of basalt, its revetments swept steeply from the featureless core. Only a single channel to break the barrier of rock, allowing passage to and from the arena. One could not arrive here but by chance. Yet here are these few, improbably settled, as though the tribe of some recondite faith, their outpost described in careless artefacts. An improvised chessboard marked out in the sand, scraps of paper pinned down as pieces. A rusted wheel raised as a miniature Colosseum, its rim anchored in gravel. Pairs of shorts and socks flapping amiably from a washing line. The diversions of men secure in their inertia.

But for himself there is no such escape. Everything is subject to conjecture. He has become lost within some vast and unfathomable puzzle, unable to deduce the design of it. Could a man be more pitifully adrift? Is it even possible to fully account the loss? A final summing of the deficit? One might devise some elementary model for it. A pie chart marked out in the sand: Volume of known fact/Volume of erased memory. Any conclusion bound of course to be flawed. One can understand oneself as a fraction only in light of the whole: quite impossible when one's mind has been sheared of vital matter.

What then is left to him in such a meagre percentage? His command over certain processes and routines seems intact – how to drive, handle a gun, and so on. And then there is that uncanny ability to recall with startling clarity excerpts from particular songs, symphonies, books or poems. But mostly there are only fragments of a former identity, discontinuous and without context, adding only to confusion.

Though at least from these there might be the beginnings of a repair. Perhaps a sequence of Bailey bridges shunted into his skull as sutures. Better still, some cordial or vitamin. Though one would first of all have to live long enough, and he has been advised otherwise.

He feels a sudden cramping in his gut. *Now!*

Swann rushes over and takes him by the arm, half assisting, half dragging him. Not, as expected, to the more private reaches of the camp but towards the rusted wheel at its centre. A black scorpion huddled within the rim, its claws lifted, its tail actuating. Something in the wind.

'So y'want to aim for that wee bastard,' instructs the lance corporal. 'Name's Rommel.' He pulls the rider's blanket away to leave him naked, then turns him so that he is facing away from the wheel. 'Come on then, one good shot t'end the whole fucken war. S'all on you.'

The rider's vision blurs. He hears encouragements to aim true. A little to the left, a step back. His bowel retches, loosing a foul-smelling stream down his legs and onto his feet. Then a further volume, causing Swann to curse and release his arm, leaving him to teeter with the force of his own evacuations. Rommel quite untouched throughout, neither advancing nor retreating.

A couple of the others have emerged from their tents, giving Swann his audience. 'Target right in his sights and he hits everything fucken but!' He brings over the can of paraffin and splashes the liquid on the rider's purpled legs and abdomen, dousing his groin, his genitals. He tosses a rag onto the rider's shoulder then walks off, shaking his head.

The rider looks down at himself, trembling. He picks up the rag and begins to wipe, but before he knows it he's weeping, his hands shaking. Why such cruelty? It's despicable, senseless. Is there nobody here to help him? He stumbles away from the wheel to cower in the shade of the Quad, where Swann brings him another blanket and a pair of sand goggles; a blasé contrition. The rider puts on both to sit in silence, frightened to cough or vomit, anything that might overtax his heart. It's the invisibility of it that terrifies. He has become a wire-walker, recognising only his height from the ground, unable to find the point of balance. Even his own filth bewildering to him. What happens to the deceased brain matter/the flotsam? Is it broken down, processed, excreted? Has he just sponged away his own memories? Shit-for-brains.

Mawdsley comes over, solicitous. He apologises for Swann's behaviour and asks if the abdominal pain has gone. This nurse who will see the sick debased. Brinkhurst fetches him some soap and water, then offers him some tinned bacon for lunch. He tells him he can return to his bed if he wishes, and the rider assents, weary of sunlight, weary of the colour red, anxious more than anything to be away from his tormentors. Helped back inside, he pulls the tent closed and tugs off the goggles to curl beneath a blanket, retreating into a cave of his own precipitous breath. If only he could be sturdier through it, weather the thing with indifference. But then who could blame him, when there is to be neither clemency nor sympathy? His muffled sobbing leading him at length to exhaustion and then to sleep, as has been prescribed best for him.

Sometimes the rider will awake at night thinking it must be day, the stillness making him fretful and unsure. At other times sleeping through daylight with a hibernatory soundness, no quantity of noise sufficient to rouse him. They come to visit him occasionally –

either Brinkhurst or the archdeacon – usually on the pretext of bringing food or drink, but more from curiosity, to see if he has recovered his memory yet, or perhaps relaxed his grip on life. Though when it begins to appear that he is not to reach either state in short order both seem to lose interest, leaving him to observe the camp from the seclusion of his hide.

It's more or less a window to absurdity. Brinkhurst busying himself with inventorying food stores while Swann will strip and clean a Bren gun, lathering gun oil on his forearms and cheeks. Or now and then joining another fellow in a spitting competition, both men positioning themselves on a hummock to hawk gobs of mucus into the breeze, whooping like children as the wind carries their best efforts across the shale. Often they will play card games, the lance corporal dragging impatiently on a cigarette while glancing wistfully to the sky, perhaps hopeful of some airborne antagonist. A dive-bomber even, that curdling fanfare of Jericho Trumpets. Anything to galvanise.

The rider counts five inhabitants of the camp in all, two still unknown to him. Other than the spit hawker, there is a skinny and unshaven fellow who keeps to himself. Dark-skinned and sunken-eyed, he wears a Bustina field cap, puttees and sturdy 'chukka' boots. Only the Italians dress so well. POW? He has that look about him, listless, beaten down. He stays mostly on the fringes of the camp, often talking to the chickens or pottering with junk from the ditch. The rider wonders if the others ever address him by name. For himself, he intends to learn the names of all here. His likely pall-bearers.

Generally the days fall into the same rhythm, the men circulatory in their distractions. Mawdsley the idler, Brinkhurst the keen-eyed administrator. While always the same exasperated impulse to adventure from Swann, the lance corporal well practised in his routine of pulling off the truck's scrim net, checking the pressures of the balloon tyres, inspecting for coolant, oil, fuel leaks. He will smear engine oil on the twin aeroscreens and throw sand on them to muddy the glaze, then pause in the cab to light a cigarette before driving from the camp without a backward glance. Each leaving effected with the same casual certainty, as though to declare it the last of his business here.

After one such departure the rider is called upon by the spit hawker, the fellow inconsiderately sloughing dust in his tent. Up close he appears to have two mouths, the lower of them a vivid weal across his chin. He shows a deck of cards. 'Pinochle? Gin rummy if you prefer. Two-player whist? I can teach you?'

'Thank you, no.'

'Name's Coates. Quinn.' He extends a hand. 'Sorry I didn't say hello before. They said you were doped.'

The rider shakes it. 'That's all right.'

'So you don't remember anything.'

'Nothing helpful.' (Can he remember whist? Gin rummy? He doesn't think so.)

'You reckon it's shock? It could be shock. There was this guy on the wheel of a twenty-five-pounder. Only one to be pulled out after an eighty-eight shell came through his crew. No idea who or where he was. Thought he was on vacation someplace. A beach break. Imagine.'

'You're American?'

'Canadian. Met my wife in Ontario, married her in Bishop's Stortford. Way before all this.' He grunts, as if acknowledging some remissness, and unbuttons his shirt pocket to pull out a folded photograph. He spends a moment in appreciation of it before passing it over.

The rider takes the photograph into his hand. A professionally taken portrait shows the Canadian in an embrace with an attractive young woman. He feels the edges of the paper, brushes the sheen of its surface. What if he were to see pictures of his own wife, fiancée or sweetheart? Subjects likely as remote to him as any characters from fiction. He glances to his own ring finger, scanning in vain for a circlet of pale skin.

He returns the photo. 'How long have you been here?'

'Myself, about three months now. The others a bit longer.'

The rider coughs, alerted once more to his vital rhythms.

'I was with the First Armoured. RASC.' Coates pulls a packet of cigarettes from his shirt and proffers one to the rider, who declines. 'The others made their way down here after Sidi Rezegh. Their units got torn up pretty bad there. Swann was a driver with the Sharpshooters, the Third London. He reckons the rest of his guys ended up POWs. Brinkhurst doesn't admit to much, but Swann reckons he was a captain with the Second Rifles. I figure Mawdsley threw in with him for the breakout.' He lights a cigarette. 'They had another guy with them at first. Cavalry guy,

Hussars. He had a bullet in his gut. Hung on for a while, but . . .'
He gestures towards the gravesite. 'Had a narrow miss myself. I
was driving a rations truck to the regiment at Agedabia when we
came up against pretty much the whole damn Afrika Korps.
Scattered us all to hell. I strayed too far south. Damn truck bust
an axle. Lucky these guys spotted me on a recce.' He breathes in
smoke. 'We don't have a working wireless here. I guess Brinkhurst
hoped you'd have news.'

'You seem well provisioned.'

'I had a full truck. We picked up some stuff from a shot-up
convoy on the way to Hakeim. We've been doing OK.' He nods
towards the chickens. 'Better than OK if you're partial to eggs.
There's stuff we can use for trade with the wogs, too. Sometimes
we can pick up supplies from killed vehicles if we head a ways
north. Fuel, ammo, med packs. Water's a bitch.'

'That's where Swann goes?'

Coates' mouths flatten as he draws on the cigarette. 'You got
old birs dotted all around here, some not on the maps. Mostly
dried up. Water's usually shit but we can try and filter it.
Otherwise it's for wash-up and the radiators.'

The rider feels a pang of envy. Swann mapping a path across
the emptiness, forearm recumbent on the door sill, skin brushed
in quartz. A bully with the blood of a pilgrim. He gestures
towards the wheel. 'He might at least take his pet with him.'

'Swann and scorpions. He hates 'em like you and me hate flies.
One stung him back at Beni Yusef and he went into shock, nearly
didn't pull through.'

The rider finds himself warming to Rommel.

'Now he's aiming to bag himself a tarantula. Or maybe some big-ass ants. Then have himself a little prize fight, take some bets.'

The rider points towards the POW. 'And him?'

'Lucky? Warrant Officer Ettore Lucchi. From Siena. He was a gunner in the Ariete Division. You ever been to Tuscany? My God, it's beautiful. He came in as Swann's prisoner.'

'He doesn't seem the type. To take prisoners.'

'There's something between them. It's personal. Who knows?' Coates catches sight of Lucchi signalling to him and waves back. 'Got a game. Let me know if you're in for a hand or two later.'

'Good luck,' says the rider, a little dismayed not to have received sympathy for his own predicament. But then perhaps it should come as no surprise, all here clearly avowed to the cause of self-interest.

The afternoon passes without incident, the air becoming static, windless, allowing the heat to build, obliging all to retire to their tents. Swann returns early from his expedition and voices concern at the stillness, judging it the precursor to some fierce storm, as is common at the close of the *Khamsin* season. Best keep an eye southward, he warns, the desert will gather there. The rider's attention meanwhile commanded by the camp's beggarly memorial, his own likely resting place. There are only shallow graves here: the sand upheaved by the wind, bones working ineluctably to the surface, depositions of knuckle, rib and longbone distributed among the minerals and glasses of whalebacks. Only those ancients deep within their caskets fortunate enough not to be cast into the sprawling ossuary. One could think of it as a kind of immortality, a perpetuity of carbonates. It makes the yearning for individuality – an identity – seem quite futile. But he can't stop thinking of the spit hawker's photograph. He can't stop thinking he might have a wife.

Later, Brinkhurst visits with a selection of clean clothing. The tent, he explains, had previously been occupied by Lucchi, the Italian having recently been bivouacked by the truck. But as the rider no longer requires undisturbed rest, they can now share. It won't be a problem.

The Italian's belongings are scant – a small Bible, a candle and holder and woollen bedroll – and he is reinstalled with a minimum of fuss, offering nothing but a polite nod throughout. When the rehousing is complete, he unfolds himself with quiet grace upon his bunk and stares upward as though the canvas might narrow to some distant window. A man withdrawn from the burdens of partisanship, decides the rider. But unsure whether to mourn the loss.

In the late evening he wakes to find the Italian scrabbling around the floor, his face a mask of dismay. He has opened the tent flaps to allow moonlight in and is using his candle as a flashlight, shading it with his hand so as not to compromise the statutory blackout. '*Il mio orologio*,' he whispers, tapping his wrist. His watch: he's lost his watch. The rider raises himself up onto his elbow and peers into the shadows, his fingers straying to his own empty wrist. Perhaps he ought to help. If he means to have any sleep, that is. But then the Italian manages to find the missing watch and holds it up in a display of relief, allowing the rider to settle again and look on with half-closed eyes as he pulls the wedding ring from his finger and places it beside the candle and the watch on a locker. When the appointed time arrives he closes his eyes and touches his breast and lips, the meaning of it undisguised. This hour stands untouched. I marry you again in the moment.

The rider shifts beneath his blanket, turning away from the ceremony, suddenly envious of his tent-mate: that he should possess such clear evidence of himself.

Tomorrow he will ask Brinkhurst for the return of his postbag. Tomorrow he will read the letters.

4

A sandstorm is coming. Swann is first to give warning, rushing into one tent after another to raise the alarm while Lucchi shakes the rider's arm to urge him from sleep, both of them hurrying outside to find the early-morning air cold and heavy, laid like a charge.

They join the others in gazing southward, where they can see beyond the ellipse of basalt a vast wall of cloud rolling towards them, chimneys of dust spiralling upward across its breadth, its hues tumbling as it gathers in the light, pinks becoming golds becoming ochres, each shift appearing to the rider as a magmatic glower. A seismicity only at this range, signalled beyond the register of the human ear, it can be no more than a dozen miles distant, billowing towards them at ungaugable speed. There's little time to prepare.

Each man hurries to his task, sealing the tents at their south-facing entrances, weighting the canvas with rocks and sandbags and opening the north-facing exits. They collect up any tools and implements lying loose, stowing or rolling them beneath the chassis of the Fordson – entrenching tools, pots and mugs, oil-cans, water cans, garments pulled from the washing line – while lesser or smaller items are left unchecked and abandoned: spark plugs, a paperback novel, muslin fuel filters, paper chess pieces. Swann throws a sheet of corrugated tin over his scorpion arena – there's to be no escape for Rommel. They fasten up the cook-house with sheets of canvas, weighting them with ammunition boxes, then Swann and Brinkhurst raise the Fordson's windows and secure the tie ropes for its tarp while Coates hauls the remainder of the corrugated sheets from the gas-burner ditch and stacks them against the Quad.

All retreat to their respective tents.

The chickens! Lucchi is first to realise the oversight and dashes from his shelter. For a few minutes he scrambles around the pen with one bird under his arm while comically pursuing its flapping companion. He thrusts both into the cab of the Fordson and races back.

The storm bears upon them as a darkening, the entire camp falling into shadow. The smaller grains lifted first, followed by the larger, as though subject to some inverted gravity, each article rived upward by order of mass. And then at once they are enveloped, a shrill canticle descending about them as the tents are snatched violently back and forth in the currents, all within obliged to shield their eyes, mouths and noses from the barrage of grit. There seems no limit in girth or weight that such a force might transport, and for a brief time each man fears being torn from his anchorage and pirouetted up into the fury.

The storm persists for several hours, the worst at last giving way to a coma of more moderate breezes, allowing the deserters to emerge from their protracted encagement. Each man beguiled now by the gentle abrasion of sand over uncovered skin.

Intent on the sensation, the rider moves to leave his tent only to be halted by a caution from Mawdsley. The shifting pressures and soiled air might overtax his lungs, he is warned, precipitating that waterless drowning, the last feeble quickening of heart muscle. As if such a thing might daunt a man whose fate has already been prescribed. What other defiance, after all, remains to him? Crouching at the exit of the tent, he lifts the blanket from his shoulders and steps out into the wind.

There is at first a moment of calm, a charitable euphoria. He stands bare-chested, his arms outstretched, his eyes closed, feeling the coolness of the air, fine sand alighting upon his skin like ash. He hangs like a puppet in the drafts, a child's idea of an aeroplane, sensing only the vestibular yaw, the loss of compass. Soon he hopes to feel the suffusing of minerals through his skin, into his bones. He might become solid before his lungs seize, before his heart stops. He might – like Lot's wife – become a pillar of salt. Or a statue of himself, a final irony.

He takes a deep breath and folds double with coughing just as Lucchi reaches him, the Italian hefting him onto his shoulder like a rolled carpet. He pulls him from the clouds and back inside the tent, where he lays him choking on the floor. The rider coughs up a slurried spit then lapses into silence, staring up at the tent's warped apex. Lucchi holding his hand, as though that small tenderness might repair him. '*Pazzo*,' he murmurs, shaking his head. Crazy.

The sandstorm persists with lesser severity into early afternoon, the sun maintaining its pallor, dense flurries stalling any excavation of the camp. For Swann the inactivity is purgatory, the lance corporal bringing his face to his tent's opening every half-hour in the hope of clearer air. The others content to wait, resigned to their enforced idleness. Other than Mawdsley, only Brinkhurst deigns to visit the rider, bringing with him the requested postbag of letters along with a roll of shaving implements and soap. A man will find his temper and self-regard improved if he attends to his appearance: it's a proven fact. The rider accepts with grace, cognisant that those tissues growing most readily will be the last to decay post-mortem: the hair, the nails. They might one day name a man from his hair.

Within the shaving kit is a mirror, which he takes up with some trepidation, viewing himself at arm's length before moving it closer. Nothing of what he sees encouraging any recall. Not the lacerated brow, the contusioned and swollen cheeks, the bearded jaw. One disguise on top of another. He might just as well study those inscrutable marbles of antiquity as discover himself in so spoilt a mask.

Brinkhurst leaves him in the company of Lucchi, seated across from him on his mattress, his field cap tight in his hands. Perhaps the Italian had expected recognition for his chivalry and is mystified at the ingratitude. If they could converse in any meaningful way they might explain one another. Instead there can only be codes and sketches, an improvised shorthand, both remaining for the most part mysterious, unable to secure any base for friendship.

The rider takes up the postbag, pausing momentarily before emptying it. For the patient whose lungs are nearing exhaustion it might be kinder to remain unknowing, reset to this blank state, insulated from grief. Were it not for curiosity . . .

He gently tips the letters onto the mattress and sorts them alphabetically: Fitzhugh (two under that name) – Hopgood-Banks – Lindqvuist (two also) – Oxburgh – Tuck (two again, but with different handwriting) – Warren. Six names in total among nine letters, nearly all belonging to soldiers of the Third Royal Tank Regiment. All of them enlisted men except for a single officer. Most are written on lightweight, self-sealing airmail letter cards, some bearing the flat-rate threepenny stamp, with several showing burn marks or dark staining. The rest penned on airgraph forms, intended to be photographed and sent in bulk as rolls of microfilm. He finds the majority of the letters unsealed, and is surprised. Has he read them already? He can't remember doing so. Brinkhurst, perhaps? That would be an unconscionable trespass, to look as a mere distraction into the thoughts of these men who have crept into trenches and turrets and turned to words as a defence.

And there is no mistaking the purpose here, even allowing for the occasional joviality or robustness of spirit among them. Each composed with thoughtful deliberation as a message of farewell. Private longings at last declared, a final invocation of hopes and wishes. Letters written in preparation for the worst, but displaying a quiet grace in the surrender.

The thought tightens his stomach: all these testimonies put somehow into his care, that fate which their authors had anticipated having presumably arrived upon them. *A postman. A great thing.*

But had that been his true office? He had worn no courier's apparel, had owned no rider's helmet. No thought or instinct of that commission ever falling upon him. Perhaps, then, one of the writers? A lone survivor? Though none of the names is familiar to him, as might be expected. So he practises for a little while in his own hand, penning examples of the upstroke, the downstroke, the cursive bridge, the arabesque, comparing each to those he finds. But nowhere among them can he see a match, his *a* not quite the same as an *a*, his *th* not matching a *th*. Could the brain when damaged possibly reassign the force and influence of each finger, the entire graphology rebalanced?

Brinkhurst returns to the tent with news. The air is clearer now, blue sky again visible, a plume of smoke sighted north of the camp. Possibly a plane crash, an unfortunate pilot caught out by the storm, obliging a reconnaissance of the site. The others are already digging out the vehicles, with Lucchi made to help. Better however for the rider to stay behind. Because he 'needs to rest' and because 'it could be a rough run'. And an enterprise ill suited to those inclined towards lackadaisical suicide.

Within twenty minutes the vehicles are ready and loaded, and the rider moves to the opening of his tent to watch as they navigate the submerged archaeology of the camp. Swann conspicuous in displaying his insignia, he notes, the others having stripped away their emblems of rank, leaving only the lance corporal certain in the idea of himself. In a more admirable soul it might be a virtue.

By the time the sound of the engines has faded, he is back among the letters, oblivious to the heat and the resurgent flies.

5

So what process for this enquiry? Where to begin?

He lays out the letters with each opening page side by side, looking at first to each greeting in the hope of a familiar endearment. *My dear/ My darling/ Sweetheart/ My beloved wife/ Dearest mother*. None pricking at his memory, each custom as impersonal to him as the next. Perhaps, then, something in the voices?

Most seem of similar character, being neither angry nor bitter in tone but offering only gentle apologies for their own end. *I am sorry this must fall upon you*, or *I fear this will put you in an awful way*, or *My regret is to have let you down*. No talk of homecoming among them, nor of reunion, but rather entreaties to fortitude, an encouragement to endure. *Please look after Mother and Father/ Your darling sister will help you through the worst/ This must not bring you to despair, Mother dear.* Others almost businesslike in addressing the matter of bequeathals, the blunt details of will and testament. *There is the remaining £1,250 from the sale of my parents' house/ My life insurance policy with Pearl/ The £26 in my Post Office Savings account.*

I could not be such a man, he decides. Not so well disposed to a cold reckoning.

Rather he finds himself drawn to those who think instead of family, ordaining their hopes and wishes for children soon to be fatherless.

I should like for him to know the countryside, to spend some time in unspoilt air ...

And,

... it would please me if he might in his studies learn something of the wider world ...

I might ask the very same things, he thinks, as this ... 'Cpl Keaton Fitzhugh', had I a son to ask them for. But how would I know? Would I remember him? One imagines such a knowledge inscribed upon one's very being, a question of spirit rather than biology.

But then had all fathers known their sons?

Thank you ...

Writes 'Cpl Graham Lindqvuist',

. . . for sending me a lock of his hair, which still surprises me for
being so fair. Though I suppose it may darken, as mine did.
Such an odd business, this choice of character. I hope you can at
least find me in those blue-grey eyes you speak of. And in other
ways as the years gather on him.

He scans for the boy's name. Ben. Benjamin. The shape and
sound of it eliciting nothing. He puts the letter aside and takes
up another, this one from a 'Trooper Edward Oxburgh' (to his
sweetheart?)

I have thought of you so very much in writing this, and have
brought the sense and picture of you so close to me that I do
not think that I can ever be put apart from you. All my
prayers . . .

A deferral to God. Could one ever forget His grace, if one had
known it? He picks another.

I must try to think of this in the best way I can – as a way to let
you know with absolute certainty that I was not afraid, and
that everything I faced here was made easier by the thought of
you with me. Throughout all you have been my best armour
and keenest sense, and my resolve here would have been by far
the poorer without you.

He composes with distinction, this ... '2Lt James Tuck'. His letter intended for ... *My Dearest Nell.*

He mouths the name.

In coming firstly to those things practical and mundane, you should know that everything I have is yours, and always has been. All monies, all possessions. I know you will make the best of all, and I hope that what sums there are will help. As to Ada, who you know is my fondest of possessions, I hope that if you decide to sell her that she will go to a good home, where she will be properly looked after. I fear she has been sadly underused by me, and ought really to be given her legs.

Beyond these, I have only the following wishes for you: that you should not be sad, or fall into despair. That you should be bold in claiming everything owed to you. I know you have the courage for this, whatever you might think. You were brave before we met and you will be brave again when I am gone. Of that I have no doubt.

He looks at the envelope side of the letter. A Midlands village. No painterly hamlet materialising, no frame over which to stitch the fabric of a memory.

He recalls another letter bearing the name of Tuck, and looks over the collection. This one sent from England addressed to the same James Tuck, written by the same Nell. Husband and wife, then. Her letter carried with him as a strength, his unhappy reply pending. The predestination of all unions hanging by words alone. Now she is husbandless, and that is the end of them.

He wipes grit from his forehead, feeling suddenly sick, in need of air. He stumbles from the tent and collapses onto his knees, aware only of his own blood and breath, the giddying rush towards extinction. Is this the moment? Should he summon strength, or resign himself? Obstinacy might only prolong the ordeal. He lowers his face to the sand, thinking at first that the hum in his ears must be a consequence of the turbulence within his own body. Some deathly current. Then he realises that the sound is outside of himself, resounding across the flat base of the arena as though from the skin of a drum. The drone of piston prop engines, their vibrations amplified between wall and rampart of the bounding rock faces. He lifts his head to see a camouflaged mono-wing aircraft make a pass over the camp, the plane low enough for the pilot's head to be visible as he leans from the open cockpit. A pale cross on its tail, black flashes in the underwing roundels.

Italian.

So they have been found.

The plane banks and climbs, then returns for a second pass. His breathlessness easing a little, consciousness no longer threatening to leave him. Perhaps not the moment, then, merely a brutal foretaste. He feels a pinch in his chest and notices the dressing beginning to darken. Should he remain still? Simply stay here on all fours for the blood to drain out? What is the pilot looking for? Have the others been captured? They should never have left him. Not in this state, weakened, defenceless. Irresponsible of them!

At last the exhaust note begins to diminish, and the rider pushes himself to his knees to watch the plane vanish. Was he seen? It's hard to be sure. Perhaps the pilot will report back his discovery and ground forces will be sent. Or a bomber despatched to level the entire camp, if they think it worth the ordnance.

He looks to the long defile that leads from the basin, the only avenue of entrance or escape. How long have the others been gone now? He has no means of telling, not even the Italian's wristwatch made available for his use. Because they think time of no consequence to him? The very opposite is true, minutes now the most precious of commodities, hours rarer still. Days he dares not even dream of. Yet here they have left him with no means to measure any. How callous. Perhaps it might be better if the Germans come. They'll have a field hospital, doctors. It might go easier for him that way. If they choose to take a prisoner, that is. Simpler in truth to make a quick end of him, to scuff the dust over a nameless body.

They should have left him a gun. Armed, he might have some power to determine his own fate. Or at least to rebuff any more counterfeit Samaritans. He lifts himself up, wincing at the pain from his battered muscles, and scans the breadth of the camp. In Brinkhurst's tent, perhaps? Items of such worth bound to be in his headmaster's care.

He makes his way unsteadily to the tent and pushes inside,

unsurprised to find its interior as insistently ordered as the man himself. Every article sited in its appropriate location, nothing laid without plan. A trellis table clothed with several maps, each carefully set at right angles to the table corners. A selection of shorts and blouses neatly piled, each garment precisely folded to preserve the seams. A partly dismantled wireless radio on a foot-locker, the handset's cord immaculately wound. He imagines that the ex-captain would use a trouser press if he had one, puffs of steam rising under the noonday sun in his toil towards impeccability. And yet he gives up the office of rank, this matron of a man, for whom order and exactitude are the keys to universal order. An unconscionable surrender.

He sees a small leather case under the bunk, and opens it to find a black Enfield revolver. He stares at the gun, as if to reacquaint himself with its purpose, then sits down to lift it, the weapon cold to the touch, as though owning its own temperature. He hefts it to shoulder height and sights down the barrel, his fingers settling to its contours in the manner prescribed by military writ . . .

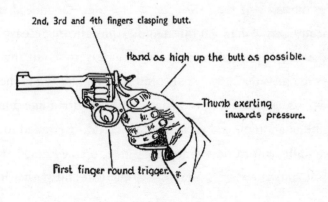

2nd, 3rd and 4th fingers clasping butt.

Hand as high up the butt as possible.

Thumb exerting
inwards pressure.

First finger round trigger.

... before tiring muscles force him to relax the pose. He unlatches the barrel, the hinged frame dropping forward to expose the cylinder's six rounds, then closes it again to re-aim, picturing Swann's face, Mawdsley's face. *If only I'd had this when that fucking German stole my watch!* But could he pull the trigger, if it came to it? Or was strength of will simply washed from his head as more functionless detritus?

He spies a large chest at the foot of Brinkhurst's bunk, its edges lined with rubber seals, and he unlatches it to find a modest trove of plunder, which he sifts through. A bottle of straw-jacketed Chianti, a bottle of Liebfraumilch (opened), a gilded alarm clock, a tin of black cherries, a box of Italian biscuits, *Prodotto di Roma*, several copies of fiction magazines: *Dime Detective*, *Hutchinson's Mystery Story*, *Phantom Detective*. He rifles through fresh undergarments, a jar of hair cream, an ivory quellazaire, an Italian medal in silver, *Medaglia al Valore Militare*. He sits back to survey the cache. So much for Brinkhurst's egalitarian collective. Do the others know? Mawdsley must at least be in on it. He and Brinkhurst perhaps spending evenings over red wine, debating the nuisance of men with mortal injuries. Or indeed of any incumbents who might threaten their government. Does Swann know? Perhaps he should.

He opens the box of Italian biscuits and bites into one, finding it agreeable – if a little stale – with a pleasant crème centre. He eats another, and then another, shedding crumbs over the bunk. Brinkhurst be damned! He gathers up the Enfield, the box of biscuits and the Liebfraumilch, then stumbles from the tent out into the middle of the camp, where he seats himself on a wooden crate to uncork the bottle. If he's behaving badly, he can't be held accountable. He shouldn't have been left. His head's not right.

Inebriated after the first mouthful, he takes up the Enfield again and sweeps the barrel in a long traverse across the hemisphere of basalt, his finger on the trigger. What a thunder he could draw! What a row! He pans the barrel back across inlets and runnels, looking for faces, familiar outlines, a worthy target. Just as a tank's gunner would, adjusting elevation, hand-cranking the turret, seeking the correct range and angle.

He lowers the gun, the effort of holding it overtaxing his arm. But there it is: logical, empirical, his foundation. He thinks like a tank crewman. He carries letters from troops in an armoured battalion. This is progress.

He stands the wine bottle in the sand and watches dully as it topples over, his head already beginning to whirl. You can't subject a failing body to alcohol! Idiot.

He stumbles back into his tent and collapses face down on his bunk, its frame spinning like a slow carousel. His hair colour: he should have logged it when he had the opportunity. He reaches out to the bundle of shaving implements left on the top of a stowage bin and seizes up the mirrored square. It's hard to look straight with the axes of his perception so askew, the gimballing failing to stabilise.

But there it is: fair hair. Red, of course, but fair if one's vision was unimpaired, as with most who are new to the desert, each inducted into that same anonymous tribe. He might once have been much darker. And his eyes? An albino red. But pale in shade, perhaps light blue or grey to those registering the full spectrum, the hue shifting depending on the character of the light, on the way it's refracted and filtered. This is how difficult it is to find yourself.

He mustn't be sick. The force of his rising gorge might overstress his heart, leaving him to decay amid the bilge of his own stomach. An idea he finds repellent but at the same time oddly amusing (that would be the wine). He drops the arm holding the mirror and gazes at the reflection of his trembling fingers. So he has imbibed himself to destruction without even learning his name. In the event, neither soldier nor scholar nor any man of discipline at all, but a mere carouser.

In the next life, he thinks, I shall be a husband and father. And that way discover myself.

He stirs to see a dim red light through the gap in the tent, the last hours of daylight now arrived, with not so much as a breeze to disturb the stillness. Groggy and beset by a vile headache, he pushes his way outside to find the camp as he had left it, wine bottle and pistol lying unburied about his makeshift seat, as though the story to some penny dreadful. His first reaction to the sight not one of relief – nor even amazement at his body's obduracy – but simply alarm. Where are they? Are they even coming back?

He confronts the thought with uncertain sentiment. No more

Brinkhurst. No more archdeacon. No more interrogation or intimidation. He has supplies of food, drugs (if he can find them), he even has a gun should he need one. But who will bury him? Is he simply to fall upon the sand at the appointed time and be gradually eroded?

He looks across to the plot of his future and fellow internee, shovelled into the ground without commendation. And yet his place has at least been marked. Pioneers might one day push into this harbour and find his gravesite. They might enter his name into their journals, restore the story of him. A fate to be aspired to.

He takes up the entrenching tool left by Swann after his post-*Ghibli* excavations, the spade parked by the petrol-fired stove. It's a mad idea. He barely has the strength, and is still suffering from the effects of his indulgences. But he must do it while he has the vim and mettle. For who else now, if not he?

He hauls the spade over to the gravesite and examines the tags looped around the crosspiece, similar to those taken from his own neck.

14026348
C   E
MOOREHEAD F

It's that easy. No burden of proof required. They will take the name and number and correlate them to an individual, and then to a family, a lineage. But the man they will find in the ground beside him, now he will be an enigma. They will have to measure his bones, gauge his teeth, gather up the residues and stains of him and subject them to the most rigorous science. But in the end they will name him, because the lure of that posthumous unveiling will be irresistible.

The surface is hard, gravel and shale now obscuring the softer ground beneath. The skin of his hands beginning to blister even after the first few strokes, barely the top layers displaced. The still potent heat obliging him to wipe sweat from his brow with each drive into the earth, his lungs unable to percolate enough oxygen into the blood. A man should not have to dig his own grave.

Overwhelmed, he sinks to his knees, surveying the stage for his funeral. There ought to be some peace to it, but rather he finds himself in the sway of despair. If he had the lungs for it, he would cry out at full voice just to hear the proof of himself. Instead he slumps forward, quite spent.

My regret is to have let you down.

It is in his peripheral vision that he first catches sight of the disturbed air rising over the basin's escape road. He peers harder, straining to distil feature and outline. Dust?

Dust!

He rises to his feet, recognising the familiar silhouettes of the Fordson and Quad travelling in line astern, the vehicles animated over the ruts and bumps. It's almost enough to make him wave madly, to bellow his gladness. But he remains still, teetering slightly over his unfinished plot, his relief as mysterious to him as it is boundless. The dour Swann at the wheel of the truck,

Brinkhurst piloting the tractor, Coates, Mawdsley, Lucchi as passengers. All present and accounted for.

He remains motionless as the vehicles steer into the leaguer and pull to a halt. Only at the last does he recall the discarded Enfield along with the looted wine and biscuits, the realisation prompting him hurriedly to collect up the evidence as the doors of both vehicles open, the occupants sombrely debussing, Swann the first to ignore him, stalking past as though he were merely another of the camp's fixtures. Then the thin-legged Brinkhurst, his jaw muscles busy in practice of some yet unspoken vexation.

'Swann! We need to talk about it. We can't just ignore it. Swann!'

The lance corporal proceeds without pause to his tent and pushes inside, leaving Brinkhurst to stand outside, hands on hips, any impulse towards a further challenge deferred. He is joined by Mawdsley, the two engaging in quiet conference. And still the rider goes unaddressed, his illicit prizes in plain sight. Coates is first to acknowledge him, offering a rueful smile as he and Lucchi begin unloading several crates from the back of the Fordson. Mawdsley breaks from Brinkhurst and the rider takes the opportunity to intercept him. 'I wondered where you'd gone. I had an attack.'

The MO pauses to register the information, then moves past the rider without further regard.

Coates and Lucchi carry the crates to the stores tent, the Italian offering the rider a quick nod as he trudges past, prompting the rider to proffer the looted biscuits. The POW stands in surprise before delving into the box, quickly eating one biscuit and sliding another two beneath his sleeve before signalling his thanks with a discreet incline of his head.

The gesture is brazen enough to catch Brinkhurst's eye, spurring him into bounding over like a maddened cricket. 'What the hell are you doing? Where did you get those things? How dare you! Is this how you repay trust? By playing the sneak thief? Is that it?'

'I wasn't sure you'd be back.'

Brinkhurst steps closer, faintly ridiculous for being the slighter man. He snatches the Enfield and depleted Liebfraumilch from the rider's hands, wincing at the bottle's lightness. 'Well, we know your colours now, don't we. Plain for all to see. Here's what we can expect!'

'I've already been told what to expect.'

'And that's a licence to thievery? That's what we deserve? Backpedalling and sneakery?'

And there's the impasse. Brinkhurst turns his attention to the Enfield, snapping the gun's breech to examine the cylinder. 'No doubt you wasted ammunition, too.'

'There was a plane.'

'Here?'

'Directly overhead.'

'Enemy?'

'Italian. Like the biscuits.'

'Were you seen?'

'I don't know. But he took a good look at the place. So that's that.'

A rude summation, but succinct. Brinkhurst spares the rider a final look of disdain and marches to Swann's tent, where he stands with unconcealed impatience. 'Swann. The plane's been over. They'll be coming. Do you hear?'

Still no lance corporal. Brinkhurst closes his eyes and drops his head. 'Swann, look. I thought you made a rash decision, that's all. Rushing ahead back there. I wasn't trying to give orders. But we need to make a decision. Swann?' He swears to himself then abandons the tent to address the others. 'This changes everything. We need to make a decision.'

Coates is slouched against the Quad. 'What's there to decide? Seems pretty straightforward. Show's over. So we head east, towards Cairo, try to make it there before Jerry. What we always said we'd do. Right?'

Brinkhurst exchanges glances with Mawdsley, neither prepared to submit their rebuttal.

'What else is there? West, and we run straight into Jerry. Probably a Kraut lockdown on Derna and Tobruk. South and we'll be dried out and dead in a week. Best way is north-east, make for Alex or Cairo.'

'That's a lot of ground to cover,' says Mawdsley.

Brinkhurst takes the prompt. 'Heavy going, mind. There might be better options.'

Coates throws his arms out. 'Like what?'

'The Akhdar mountains are about a hundred and fifty miles

north-west of here. That's a third of the distance to Cairo. Couple of days' travel should see us there. Somewhere to regroup, take stock.'

Coates eyes move from one to the other. 'We're here because it was this or a lot worse. Anybody would do the same. But what you're talking about, that's different. That's a whole other thing.'

'We make the best decision we can under the circumstances. What use are we dead or captured?'

'And you think a military court would go for that? 'Cause the last I heard, they were talking about trotters being given the bullet.'

Brinkhurst lifts his chin. 'We have a wounded man with us.' (The rider is indignant to find himself singled out.) 'We do what we can. We take the most reasonable option. Can't put a man on a charge for that.'

'Say what you want. No way am I gonna vote to run. I'm saying it right now. So that we're straight.'

The stand-off is broken by Swann, who emerges from his tent and strides to the petrol oven, where he squats to turn on the fuel tap.

'What do you say, Swann?' asks Brinkhurst, pointedly deferential.

'Hungry as fuck.' The lance corporal pulls a lighter from his shorts and ignites the pooling reservoir of fuel.

Brinkhurst takes a breath, relieved to find their feud in abeyance. 'All right, but let's go steady on the fuel, shall we? We're going to need it.' He directs his attention to the rider. 'The filchers and pilferers among us can retire for the evening.'

The rider withdraws, slogging back to his tent along with the equally criminalised Lucchi. Why should he care? It doesn't matter where they run to, his fate will likely be the same. Death by suffocation, either in this miserable lair or in the baking cargo bed of a truck. No preferred scenario for him except the hope of a quick end, of being felled suddenly and without warning. That would be his prize of choices. And after he is gone? Then let the world burn.

6

Back in their tent Lucchi sits opposite the rider, his mouth turned down in comradeship. The Italian retrieves the extra biscuits from his sleeve and leans across to offer one. The rider accepts it and nods in the direction of the voices outside, his arms spread in a gesture of enquiry. What happened?

Lucchi gathers up several implements to use as characters: Brinkhurst (he pronounces it *Breenkoowursse*) played by a comb, the role of Swann taken by the candle. He picks up one of the rider's pieces of paper and folds it into a crude aeroplane for his third protagonist: '*Italiano.*' He clears a space in the sand and scores out a rough circle, placing at its centre a crumpled sock. '*Il luogo dell'incidente.*' The crash site. He proceeds to act out a small theatre, the comb and candle edging towards the sock then pulling back again as the paper aeroplane swoops over. The candle finally making a break for the centre just as the paper plane passes overhead, both freezing in reaction to one another. He concludes the act by picking up the comb and standing it on its end, making it violently hop. '*Questo e tutto.*'

The same spotter plane, then, as that which overflew the camp, the pilot now able to report both the base and its vehicles. Little wonder at Brinkhurst's dismay.

Lucchi makes several further attempts at conversation, his conviviality perhaps encouraged by the possibility of rescue. When finally the Italian settles to private contemplations, the rider ignores the discussion outside to delve back into the postbag, searching for that one anomalous entry to the canon, that one letter written by a wife to her husband. (To be kept only by he who might hold it dear?) He takes it to the opening of the tent and into the light of the moon, where he stares at the name, finally daring to voice it beneath his breath.

Nell. The medieval 'Mine El' contracted, Eleanor in the formal. The poetic declension, elocuted open-mouthed, chiming from the palate. Such a happy phonetic might pretend at memory.

Dearest Husband,

I was so thankful to receive your last letter, and relieved to hear that you are well and in good spirits. Receiving it was such a boost that it made me quite dizzy, and I carried it in my pockets for the entire week. I swear there's a healing power to such things.

It is cold here now. We have a hard frost most mornings, and sometimes thin ice on the window panes. Some say it must snow soon. The other morning the stirrup pump froze over and several of us had to attack it with tools to unblock it. Fortunately I was able to buy a winter coat very recently from our machine setter at the factory, Mr Heyse, whose mother sadly passed away earlier this year. I'm afraid I look rather a fright in it but it was certainly a bargain and keeps me quite warm. Though I do think that anyone looking out of their window that morning must have been alarmed to see a grizzly bear with a hammer.

I made another visit to Dr Franklyn at his Walsgrave Road surgery last week, and I know it will cheer you enormously to hear that he described my health as 'capital' (who uses such a word now but doctors and bankers!) Of course I am still to avoid the cold and damp (which I am more than glad to do) but I am doing very well now, with my chest trouble far less worrisome than before. As I should be delighted not to see the old humbug again for the duration of the war, this is better than splendid news.

I'm sure you will be almost as pleased to know that I managed to wheel out Ada and take her for a run the other day. Just to stir the oil and keep her in fine fettle, as you asked. Not very far of course, just through the village (I tried not to go too fast this time!) but I think she enjoyed her outing. Petrol is impossible to get now and she is running low, so there may not be many more of these excursions.

*Though I'm sure our neighbour Mrs Galloway will be only
too pleased, as she complains Ada's exhaust is loud enough to
raise Cain.*

*Generally I am doing well, and want for nothing except your
soonest return, so you mustn't worry on my account. The time
spent waiting for your messages is the most difficult, and there
isn't a morning that I wake without wondering whether I shall
hear from you that day.*

Thinking of you every moment.

With all my love,

Nell

xxx

xx

It's possible now to compile a roster of detail, facts that might
elicit some recall:

   i. She is a machinist, a factory worker.

  ii. She rides her husband's motorcycle. (A motorcycle because
     'wheeled out'?)

 iii. She is alone, with no mention of friends or family.

 iv. She suffers from some chest trouble, which has given cause
    for concern.

Except that he feels no rush of familiarity. Perhaps because
he has misconceived the damage to his brain. One thinks of

memories as being diffuse, their signal being enrooted over such an area as might deny clean excision. But perhaps not so?

He would consider the principle at greater length but for the tiredness that weighs upon him. It's been a day of industry, Liebfraumilch, crème biscuits and gunmanship, and altogether too much for a dying man. Nevertheless, in that state of semi-delirium there is a scene which becomes briefly open to him: a vast hall ceilinged with conduits, vents and umbilicals, its floor decked with engines, wheels and cranks, as though the helm to a twoscore of ships. She stands in the centre on wooden duckboards, fragile against the pipes and gears of monstrous engines: planes, shapers, angle-grinders, petrol-engined 'boneshaker' lathes harnessed to a single spinning axle. She is slight in build, modestly arresting in feature, her hair dark in the green-hued neon under which she toils. One of many working in isolation, fastidious in mounting the pieces to the post of her lathe, cranking them forward by microincrement to be fashioned and finished. Her overalls sodden down one side from the suds sprayed to cool the workpieces, oil smeared on her cheek where she will intermittently wipe the back of her hand. He can see that she is careful and confident with those instruments presumed the equipage of men: hacksaw, rule, micrometer, spanner, wrench, eighth gauge, the Vernier protractor. And in the buckets at her feet the results of her industry: pivot pins, spools, tapered sockets, spigots, ferrules, washers, nuts, screws, bolts. In the hangar beyond they are assembling a bomber for which she has crafted the parts. And when complete, she will spare a moment of elation at it, as the means by which she might save her husband.

The noise is ferocious, each woman contesting the whine of gears with her own song or mantra, so that when the machines cease abruptly at the letter bearer's entrance, there lingers for an instant a profound and dissonant chorale. This too dying to leave the bearer navigating the aisles in silence, postbag across his shoulder, watched in awe by all. Until finally he arrives at her station, there to deliver to her a letter the rider imagines marked exactly so . . .

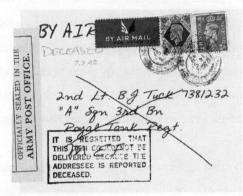

. . . this slender deposition completely breaking her.

He awakes with a start to find Brinkhurst sitting opposite, Lucchi now absent. Alarmed, he lifts himself to an upright position.

'I sent Lucky for a walk.' Brinkhurst scratches at his forehead, an arc of paler skin prefiguring thinning hair. The rider has never guessed at his age before. Late twenties, early thirties? Perhaps nearer forty. Men of his cast seem to have only one predetermined age, which settles upon them in youth. The brigadier gene.

'Look, I don't see you as a problem,' the ex-captain begins. 'I don't want to see you as one. Swann . . .' he scratches his jaw, as though irked by the wilful muscle there '. . . Swann is necessary. He's good with the vehicles and knows the country. But with a man that undisciplined you run against the odds every day. Because he will just incessantly push his luck. And ours. We simply can't allow ourselves to be ruled by that kind of behaviour.

'Now your fellow Coates. He's another case altogether. A thinking man, but misguided. This idea he has of rejoining our lines, it's complete folly. Travelling that kind of distance across open desert with limited supplies. We might have the fuel, but what about water? What if the vehicles break down? In the middle of nowhere? What then?'

The rider leans to meet Brinkhurst's gaze. 'My lungs are going to fail.'

'That's Mawdsley's opinion. But what do you say? Do you think he's right?'

The rider hesitates, disarmed.

'I mean, do you feel worse? Do you actually sense yourself becoming worse?'

'I've been told it will happen.'

'Yes, but you're alive, aren't you? And you'll probably be alive tomorrow morning. And the morning after. And the one after that. So when will it come to that morning that you're not alive? Did he tell you that? Did he give you that time? A week? A month? A year?'

The rider feels his balance beginning to drift. What is he being told?

'Mawdsley is a fine medic' – the words chosen with care – 'but out here in the field it's a case of best guess. He's given an opinion, and you've accepted it.' He softens his tone. 'The mind can heal the body. I've seen it myself, even from the most terrible injuries. It happens.'

The rider wishes he had the Enfield again.

'Look, you're one of the group, and you have a vote. Nobody will deny you that. And you need to consider your choices. It's a question of which option gives you the best chance. Trekking across an empty desert or moving to an environment where you can rest and recover.'

So there it is: he is to be recruited. Signed into an inner cabal, among men who have run from their comrades, who are at ease with the idea of schism. 'You've put it to the vote?'

'We'll do it at first light. And then we'll move. At the moment it looks like three to one in favour of making for the Jebel. Coates is against it. But I know him, he'll work on Swann. There'll be a split tomorrow. It'll come down to you.'

The rider drops his head. Under different circumstances the thing might be farcical. 'What does Swann want?'

'To not be commanded. Or instructed. Or advised.'

'He might have chosen a better career.'

'Oh, he likes the army well enough. He just doesn't want anybody else in it.' Brinkhurst rises and straightens his shirt. 'Mawdsley and I, we'll see you right. We won't dismiss you. I hardly think you can expect the same of Swann. I think you've seen that already.'

He pauses at the sound of someone outside the tent, then relaxes when Lucchi nervously enters, the Italian remaining on his feet until directed to sit. 'You're perhaps thinking there's some kind of leadership quarrel,' the ex-captain adds in afterthought. 'But you shouldn't.' He bends to leave. 'Because there is no effective chain of command out here. None at all.'

And then he is beyond the mouth of the tent and gone.

Lucchi throws a questioning look, enquiring with gestures on the nature of the visit. '*Un grande segreto?*' But the rider dismisses him, still distracted by Brinkhurst's intrigues. What after all is he supposed to believe? That he might not die? That some miraculous rehabilitation awaits if he should fall in with the right group? A ruthlessness – beyond cruel – to even taunt him with the possibility.

Further attempts by Lucchi at conversation prove futile, and the Italian succumbs eventually to his tiredness, leaving the rider to consider those imponderables that have narrowed almost to an obsession: the volume of air he is able to draw in, the efficiency of gaseous exchange, the inexorable reduction in oxygenated blood. Reclining to stare into the dark, he imagines himself finally as some great whale spiralling to the depths, engorged with air, knowing then that he cannot drown.

7

There is a mist at daybreak, steamed from moisture condensed during the cold of night, which has settled about the basin of the camp. At first light a marvel, the entirety of the barricading rock dissolved. And for the rider, entering the clouds from his tent, a melancholy wonder, invoking notions of an ocean yet to be desert.

The last to awake even at this early hour, he finds the others already busy: Mawdsley stacking blankets and clothing outside the tents, Lucchi rehousing the chickens in a wooden cage, Coates dismantling the petrol burner. Brinkhurst ever the ring-master, clipboard in hand. Have they taken the vote? Is it decided?

Swann emerges from the thinning mist, notebook in hand. 'Umpty. Got a job for you.'

'I haven't eaten yet.'

'This first. Be quicker with two.'

The lance corporal leads him to the cookhouse, a single tarpaulin sheet rigged outside it to give shade to a hodgepodge of tins, boxes and packets. He hands the rider a pencil and the notebook, opened to display a handwritten inventory. 'Need to check what's here against what's written down, make sure it's right. So that Cap'n Tightarsed over there can work out the rationing.'

The rider nods, glad at last to be involved. He reads the first few entries – 15 tins of bully ✓ 9 tins of Carnation ✓ 8 tins of biscuits ✓ 2 half-sacks of tea ✓ 12 tins of M & V skilly ✓ – and watches as Swann pulls out the respective stocks.

'Is it decided where we're going?'

'Green Mountain.'

5 packets of Italian dried minestrone ✓ 1 sack of sugar ✓.

'It's certain then?'

'Oh, I'm sorry, were you not asked?'

'I thought Coates had a different idea.'

Swann grunts as he hefts the sack of sugar. 'What d'you care what Coates thinks?'

'Brinkhurst said there'd be a vote.'

The lance corporal drops the sack and straightens himself. 'A vote? That's nice. Not much sense voting on the dead fucken obvious, is there? Next.'

8 tins of sardines ✓ 4 tins of marmalade ✓ 1 wrap of German rye bread ...

'Scratch that,' orders Swann on peeling open the foil. 'Fucken bug food.' He lobs the bread beyond the camp's perimeter. 'So Brinkhurst's got you on his team now, eh? Goin' to elect you to his war council?'

'I don't know.'

'Told you some shite about me, didn't he? I knew he would.'

The rider fumbles for a deflection.

'Bet I know what he didn't tell you. About the guy he brought with him when he came here. A tankie, Seventh Hussars, from Sidi like the rest of us. Poor bastard had taken a round through the gut. Looked for a while like he might make it but he kept shittin' blood, shrunk away to nothin' in the end. And you know what he said? About your new best pal there? That Brinkhurst had his unit fire on our own boys. That he panicked, just gave the order and didn't give a fuck. That's your great leader for you.' He nods towards the gravesite at the camp's perimeter. 'So you reckon he got offered a vote too?'

The rider notices that Brinkhurst has his eye on them from the far side of the camp.

Swann steps closer. 'If you want my advice, you'll watch your back with him. Him and his bloody pet quack.'

The rider looks again to Brinkhurst, now turned to some other business. To what purpose, then, the persuasion of last night? As a test of loyalty, a means of consolidating his influence? 'How many are these supplies meant for?' he asks, alarmed at his own question.

'As many as there's left to eat 'em,' says Swann.

And there is the truth of it, adroitly touched. A man in his position can neither give nor expect loyalty. Yet he is forced nonetheless to an allegiance, two such as Brinkhurst and Swann bound eventually to contest one another. The invidious choice of bully or conniver as confederate.

'I'll look out for you if you'll do the same for me,' he blurts, already mustering himself for the rebuff.

Swann glares at him then hocks up a gob of spit. 'Better finish that list.'

The rider nods, relieved. So it's done. He's thrown his lot in. This is your strength. This is how you survive. He looks across the camp, wondering if Brinkhurst is watching again, but finds the ex-captain's attention commanded now by something new: a low hum resounding from the encircling rock, the frequency of it relayed like current across the stadium's base.

Brinkhurst's skyward gaze gives cue for the others to do likewise, their dismay mirroring his own. By the time the plane materialises, etching itself as a slender dihedral against the dawn light, there is little to do but run. *Getdowngetdownrungetinthetrenches!* Swann barges past the rider to head for his tent while Brinkhurst makes for the slit trenches. Coates scans frantically for cover before rolling under the Quad. A startled Mawdsley emerges from his tent only to dart back inside.

The plane descends a parabola of air, feathers of mist pluming at its wingtips. The rider hears somebody telling him to run. He's not sure whose voice it is. Coates? Where is there to run to? He can't even run, for God's sake.

The fighter's cannon bursts into life, the rounds punching up brumes of grit, the sound shifting to a cacophonous rainfall as they strike metal: the Fordson, the Quad, the fuel burner, the Colosseum. The rider makes to enter the shelter of the cookhouse but thinks better of it, repelled by the thought of shrapnel spat from food tins.

The plane completes its first pass and swoops upward, banking to begin the next run. Swann races back into the clearing carrying the Bren. He slams the machine gun's bipod across the engine cover of the Fordson and thrusts in the curved magazine, pulling back the bolt as the plane begins its approach. He stabs the fire button, the Bren's chatter starting up in flat counterpoint to the cannon.

The rider feels a rush of pressure across his chest, the sensation quickly becoming a searing pain. But no blood, no broken skin. Too much for his weakened heart, then. He collapses to his knees, and then onto his side, a gaffed fish. He can hear only the roar of his own blood, see nothing above the thinning cumulus but the black dorsal of the Bren.

The air clears a little to show Swann mouthing some oath, then thickens again. The rider rolling onto his back as a series of dry geysers spouts at his side. Such a simple thing to raise himself up, present himself as a target, bring the thing quickly to its finish . . .

He turns his head to see Coates emerge from beneath the Quad, his face and forearms thick with powder. The Canadian stands in a whorl of sand to pull open the vehicle's cab door, and drags out a swathe of pale fabric. He holds up the material with both hands.

Another wave of pain engulfs the rider's breast, the shock of it causing him to retch. Still he remains conscious, the agony once more receding. The camp a blur now, the image of a fluttering red cross insistent. Coates at once formless and refigured, swimming upward but never surfacing. He thinks Swann is no longer firing the Bren, and that the plane has ceased its attack, but he is somewhere between those worlds within and outside of himself, certain of nothing. He dares to take a deeper breath and shifts his head a fraction, seeking to move it from the pooling bile beneath. He hears the plane's exhaust note deepen and increase in volume. And still Coates persists with his banner. Clever, he thinks, to signal the camp as a medical station. Quite desperate.

Coates holds his ground. It seems almost an unfairness when the plane's cannon barks into life at the last, kicking up a series of flumes around him as he drops the banner and lunges to his right. The rider thinks he sees something separate from the Canadian's face and spin away into the sand. How sad, he muses: that the spit hawker has lost his mouths.

The plane returns once more, a crescendo of rent metal rising. Someone is sobbing, blubbering. It's all beyond him now. You did really well, they might have said, had he been sympathetically attended. To hold on as long as you did.

Though in truth, if he had known surrender to be so easy, he might never have endured the struggle.

8

It is the sense of movement that rouses him. Draughts stirred by those passing close by, the career of shadow and light. Then the sound of voices raised in dispute, as though echoes of some distant commotion.

He opens his eyes to find himself beneath the canvas of a fetid arbour, a cloud of flies settled about him, their legs and mouths probing every inch of exposed skin. Too great an exertion to swat them away, his limbs no longer his own. He can smell stale vomit on his chest, taste it between his teeth. He turns his head to see he has a neighbour propped upright on a bunk several feet distant, the fellow's head and neck parcelled in gauze, a length of slick tubing drooping from his throat, the flies gathered to him in such numbers that his head appears daubed with a living tar. Some funerary pavilion, where the dead and almost dead are laid in readiness, the organs to be removed, the body desiccated and enswathed to go before the sternest of judges. He-whose-Eyes-are-in-Flames, The Breaker of Bones, The Eater of Entrails, He-who-does-not-allow-Survivors.

A face looms close. We'll be leaving soon. You should try and stay awake.

He-who-brooks-no-Dissension, The Purveyor of Mistruths.

Try and stay awake. He closes his eyes again, preferring sleep.

Cairo! That tumbledown Babylon, palace of effluvial airs, rank with the swill of a thousand cuisines. Mother of the World, as the Sassanids would have it. He is caught up in the old pandemonium, the squeal of tramlines, the fanfare of horns from taxis, buses, trucks, horse-drawn gharries vying for street inches with bullock-carts, touts, pedlars, beggars, loafers, bootblacks, dragomans. *Hotel reservation, effendi? Diamond bracelets, effendi – only the finest! Bath mats of Nile reeds, amulets from the tombs of the Pharaohs* (MADE IN BIRMINGHAM). *One night of bliss, brave soldier-pasha! One night of heaven with my radiant and virginal sister.*

He pauses before the Cinema Metro, its hoarding promoting **FLIGHT COMMAND**. Ens Robert Taylor redeemed in the eyes of his fellow navy fliers, having saved the skin of Sqn Cdr Walter Pidgeon. *You're a born hellcat, pal, and we're gonna hang on to you!*

He has boot polish splashed onto his shins and a coronal of flaming poinsettias thrust under his nose. He acquires his own jester draped in bead necklaces – hands laced with strings of glass spittle – who clears his path with a jig. *Pearls of the Nile, effendi. Glory of the Sultans!*

He wanders on, leaving the wider avenues for a hive of flat-roofed dens, humble caves of stucco, *malqaf* wind scoops infusing their cores with the cooler breezes, the air between them heavy with the stink of raw effluence, tobacco smoke, burnt rice. He passes *fellaheen* reposed on palm leaves, children squabbling over dried camel dung. Somewhere in this tawdry theatre are the gates to himself, a great temple of proof lying just beyond his reach. That much he is sure of. That much he remembers. But the metropolis is overwhelming, engulfing, rising up in its noise, heat and dust, leeching vitality, infusing torpor.

Only from the rooftops is there a sense of rapture, of divination. The Blue and White Niles conjoined to a single aortic, pulsing though the Sudan, through Luxor, Aswan, rushing continental floodwaters to the Delta. The great Moqattam cliff, rising like a portcullis over the City of the Dead, unfurling its sun-flayed land eastward out to the Red Sea, to Bible lands. It is all relinquished earth, the will of some great tellurian force.

His search for himself, he realises, could be ageless.

'Damned lucky.' Mawdsley pushes against his shoulders, forcing him back onto his haversack pillow, flies glued to the mucilage of his neck. 'That's what you are.' The MO gazes at him with blood-threaded eyes. 'We all thought you'd had it. I mean properly had it.'

Obliged to stillness, the rider surveys the tent, recognising it as the same occupied by he and Lucchi, its interior now stripped to an austere ward.

'How's your breathing?' asks the MO. 'Any pain?'

You always ask that.

The rider looks again to his fellow patient. 'Coates?'

'He was hit in the face. His jaw's gone. Left ear, too. Bone fragments in one eye. It's not savable. Look, we're going to be pulling out soon. I'll come and get you when we're ready.' He rises and moves to the tent's entrance. 'You'll need to watch him, make sure his head stays upright. Listen for any sounds of choking. There might be teeth fragments.' He pauses. 'He doesn't know.'

He exits the tent, leaving the rider anxious and unsettled. Too easy now for his accomplices to slip away, abandoning him and Coates to a certain end. Exhaustion, creeping infection, starvation. Execution perhaps, if the enemy deigns to visit.

Coates looks to him and makes a feeble gesture, two fingers held aloft then brought close to his bandaged face. A smoke. A cigarette, for God's sake. The rider looks at the linen about the Canadian's head, that sudden cliff where the wrap should follow the contour of a chin. He levers himself gently from his bunk and wades across on his knees, the skin surrounding the spit hawker's uncovered eye pruning as he repeats his signal.

The rider shakes his head. 'Doctor's orders.'

Coates uses his right hand to simulate the act of writing, prompting the rider to look to the postbag at the foot of his bunk, the writing implements scattered nearby. He passes an envelope and pen over and affects patience while Coates grapples with them.

DONT LEAVE ME HERE

'They won't. They won't do that, I promise. I'll go and see Brinkhurst now.'

He moves from Coates' side to shuffle his way to the entrance of the tent, then pushes out into the sunlight, the sight of a levelled camp surprising him. The other tents struck, the washing line and clothes removed, the fuel-burning oven dismantled, the cookhouse demolished, its stores depleted.

Brinkhurst looks up from his seat on a nearby ammo crate. 'That a good idea? Dragging yourself around like that?'

The rider leans back on his haunches, catching his breath as Brinkhurst directs his attention to the far side of the camp, where Swann is rummaging in the junk pit, his forearms black with oil as he lifts then discards axles, carburettors, broken tools, empty cans. Brinkhurst points towards the rusted amphitheatre, now shot through by cannon fire. 'Rommel's cleared off.'

The rider takes his eyes from Swann. 'Coates needs a hospital.'

'Mawdsley tells me the wound will fester within a day.'

'We could leave him for the Germans.'

'The Germans, yes. If they come. But if they do, don't you think he'd give up everything he knows about us? For the promise of help? I know I would.' He pulls off his cap and uses it to bat at flies. 'We'll be moving out soon, so gather whatever you need. Don't worry about Coates, Mawdsley will see to him.'

Swann hurls a broken shovel into the pit. He strides back into the centre of the camp and proceeds to lift the sheet of corrugated tin from the oven trench and flip it over. Brinkhurst shades his eyes. 'Swann, for God's sake. Why don't you try burning him out? Use the dirty petrol. Mawdsley can help.' He signals to the MO, who seems uncommonly agitated, his eyes repeatedly scanning the grounds of the dismantled camp as though unable to take any register of it. He walks to a pile of jerrycans and picks one out marked with a black X.

The rider watches him, fascinated. 'Is Mawdsley all right?'

'It's the Benzedrine. He'll calm down shortly.'

'He's a doper?'

'Hardly the worst of vices. Your friend Swann is a far greater liability. Not that it stopped you from running to him, did it? To make your little alliance.'

The rider is dumbfounded. 'I didn't . . .'

Brinkhurst offers him a look of charity. 'We really shan't get along if you try to put things over on me. It's not a gentleman's way at all. Don't you agree?'

Chastened, the rider defers. Brinkhurst the gamesman, casually shuffling the truth. A lesson not easily forgotten. He watches as Swann directs Mawdsley to the remains of the cookhouse, the MO using his lighter to ignite the petrol.

Brinkhurst rises. 'Thank heaven. We'll be leaving in five minutes. Make sure you're ready.' He heads off towards the Fordson.

The rider looks on as Swann and Mawdsley continue at their ritual, the bounds of the camp now demarked by pillars of flame. He turns away to re-enter the tent, where he finds an increasingly discomfited Coates, the Canadian now more alert to his injury, his hands busy around the hole in his throat.

The rider goes to his side. 'We're making for Cairo. There'll be aid stations. A hospital.'

Coates looks at him and blinks, then grips his shoulder. An ordainment, more or less.

The leaving preparations are concluded in an atmosphere of fragile calm, the last remaining tent struck by Brinkhurst and Lucchi, the rider and Coates assisted by Mawdsley to a den of blankets in the cargo bed of the truck. Coates is administered a further ampoule of morphine and is equipped with a grease pencil and sheet of tin cut from a petrol can as his means of communication. No one – under the circumstances – thinking the stench of fuel a penalty. Swann loads the last of the provisions aboard the truck before making the usual mechanical checks: balloon-tyre pressures, oil, amperage reading, fuel-tank seals, coolant level. On discovering a holed radiator for the Fordson, he reports the finding with an expletive then proceeds to break open two eggs and crush them into the coolant reservoir, warning that the boiled whites will dam the breach only so long. Of the truck's overladen bed – the rider, Lucchi and Coates now installed beneath the canopy bows – he makes only the comment 'too fucken heavy', slapping his palm against the hardwood boards to underscore it.

A short conference brings proceedings to a close, Brinkhurst laying out maps across the engine panels of the truck for him and Swann to study. The lance corporal sets a brass sun compass for a northwesterly bearing and affixes the device to the dash of the Fordson. He slides into the truck's driving seat while Brinkhurst takes his place beside Mawdsley at the wheel of the Quad, both men firing up the engines.

The rider grabs for the side as the Fordson lurches forward, the slumped Coates against his shoulder, Swann's face leant from the cab window as they motor from the camp. Still scouring, thinks the rider, for that skitter of legs, the familiar tail ratcheted into a question mark. *Is that the best you can do?*

Cowards!

Two

9

They journey through the morning, maintaining good pace where the going is not too soft, wary of sending up any signal of their travel. Past the downed plane, its fuselage lodged like some ossified longbone into the crust. Then beneath a sequence of rubblestone spires, each higher than its neighbour, the colonnade opening onto a field of volcanic clinker, black boulders piled as though to serve some ancient cannonry. All the while navigating with caution the thinly crusted salt pits that pretend at solid earth. Every half-hour Swann pulls the truck to a stop and takes a fresh magnetic compass bearing from a northwesterly landmark, then re-orients the vehicle towards it before adjusting the direction needle of the sun compass. Each time the entire procedure executed without remark. On the fourth stop Brinkhurst climbs from the Quad and studies through binoculars the ground ahead, referring to his map for confirmation. They're nearing the first of a number of desert trails, he explains. Al Tariq al Abd, Al Tariq Anwar, Al Tariq Bir al Hakeim. Rough desert trackways, most of them old trading routes, their sand and gravel compacted by the passing of merchant trains, the barefoot marches of slaves. And now channels for the transportation of troops and armour across open desert. The trail they are approaching appears empty but they'll need to remain vigilant for any sign of hostile forces. Or just as calamitously, their own.

Brinkhurst steps back into the Quad and starts the engine, leading both vehicles off at slow speed. Their leaving distantly observed by a pair of long-eared desert foxes from the top of a ridge, each party regarding the other with incredulity. *What are you about? Who put you here?* These and other nightbound creatures thrown from their habits by evenings made bright by flares and tracer, by days blackened with oil smoke. What a feat, marvels the rider, to come into this vastness and confuse nature.

A little nearer the trail they see that the ground has been littered with the vestiges of an army in transit. Shell casings, empty ration tins, a length of tank track, an oil drum set as a waypost. A domed shape they take to be a solitary cairn is revealed at closer range to be a man folded over his stomach, white with dust and long dead. The rider doesn't recognise the uniform – French? But why no burial? Perhaps he had wandered here on his own having made his escape from battle, then succumbed while awaiting traffic, one of his fingers pointed west as though to indicate his preferred direction of travel.

The trail still clear, Swann and Brinkhurst gun the vehicles, the truck bouncing violently over the lip of a crater before crossing its flat surface. The rider moves once more to prevent Coates toppling, the Canadian awake now that the morphine has exhausted its potency. He lifts his tin message board to scribble:

SICK

The rider hauls himself to his knees and leans forward to beat on the fabric of the truck's cab. 'Swann! We need to stop!'

The lance corporal continues to drive at speed, following the Quad's tyre tracks as both vehicles bounce and jolt over a rugged floor. Only when they have driven far enough to put the cover of a limestone hillock behind them does he snake the vehicle to a halt and step in fury from his seat. 'Are you fucken stupid?' and, 'Don't ever do that again unless you see a fucken mine!'

The rider sees Brinkhurst and Mawdsley hurrying from the parked Quad. 'We have to get the bandages off. He's going to be sick.'

Mawdsley unlatches and drops the truck's tailgate. He clambers into the cargo bed and begins quickly unwrapping Coates' face and neck, the task only just completed before the Canadian leans forward to retch, a glimpse of his jawless mouth enough to turn the rider's stomach. He pushes himself from the cargo bed to alight upon the shale then stumbles a little way from the truck, his bruised muscles stiffened, his skin tightened where the abrasions have begun to scab. He rubs his bare legs where the muscle is most stubborn, and notices a bleached chevron of skin. A burn mark or scald, seemingly older than other wounds. He runs his fingers over its glassed surface, hoping to tease out the story of it. The artefact, perhaps, of some defining episode. He should ask Mawdsley about it. Mawdsley will set him straight.

Brinkhurst announces their imminent departure, and the rider remounts the cargo bed to take his place beside a freshly bandaged Coates, the Canadian now equipped with an additional throat tube by which to receive fluids. After a brief consult of their maps Brinkhurst and Swann resume their drivers' positions in the vehicles, and within minutes they are under way again.

The rider watches Coates totter against the boards, death surely now mantled about him. Yet in his dulled gaze there is still the hope of escape. Some miracle that might see him vault from the truck to hit the sand sprinting, leaping dunes and wadis, the lint on his face unbinding as he runs, the bone and tissue beneath bonded by action of the breeze. Until at last he might arrive at the sea cliffs fully restored, and from there force his way against the tide, out to anchored battle cruisers whose sailors might net him in and set him to his voyage home, returning him finally to his house and to the arms of his wife – exactly as in the photograph – who might throw herself about his neck and weep with gladness and ask of him: 'How, my love, did you ever make such a return?'

To which he might reply: it was what was owed to us.

The spit hawker lays his hand over the rider's, his fingers flecked with bile.

The rider squeezes his arm. Try to hold on.

They journey onward, the sun risen now to its noon height, pulling up shadows like drawbridges, rendering the sun compass useless. They drive across an acreage of red serir dotted with gazelle bones. Then over a wide scapula of limestone, erupted here and there into solid vortices, as though a vestigial geography had in one instant been pulled skyward then denied. They skirt the husks of long-exhausted volcanoes and their fields of pumice to emerge onto a gypsum crust, its tablets and plinths upended and see-sawed in the manner of a fissured floe. Until they come presently to an immense platform of sand and shale over which are strewn a number of derelict fighting vehicles, each so brutally razed that a great scarp of fire might have slid across the desert, rapacious of all before it.

The Fordson and Quad draw to a stop, Swann joining Brinkhurst in the study of a partially unfolded map. Brinkhurst raises his binoculars. 'Looks like armoured divisions. Can't be more than a couple of days old. Christ. Whole bloody thing's been right on our doorstep.'

Swann points out a truck nosed into the gravel. 'One or two soft skins about. Maybe worth a look-see.'

'Might still be recon patrols in the area,' says Brinkhurst. 'Safer to just push on, put some distance into it.'

The lance corporal sullenly resumes his driver's seat, both vehicles moving off in tandem. The rider raises himself up to watch, holding onto the truck's sideboards as it motors past dugouts and trenches, bouncing every now and then over shallow runnels scored by the vacuum of low-trajectory shells. They draw by an upended and buckled twenty-five-pounder gun, now resembling the caricature of a plough. Then past a gutted 'Honey' tank, the end of its gun barrel opened like a daylily, a scatter of black berets laid on the surrounding sand, their owners seemingly dropped straight as plumb bobs into the ground. Occasionally the rider will spy a corpse laid out beside the wreckage of a vehicle, the bodies either exposed to the wind or hurriedly sheeted over. Those men abandoned or forgotten, now given up to the scoria of rock and bones. Will anybody seek them out?

He ducks on hearing a sudden tearing noise, then grabs Coates' arm and pulls him down among the cans and boxes as splinters of wood blast up from the truck's boards, the caged chickens flapping in alarm. Brinkhurst slews the Quad to a halt, and he and Mawdsley drop from the cab to roll into the sand, the vehicle shuddering at the impact of rounds along its length. Swann drives the truck level with the Quad then opens the door and throws himself out. He scurries to the cover of its left-side front wheel, Brinkhurst and Mawdsley worming on their elbows and stomachs to join him.

The rider wipes splashes of petrol from his cheek. Should he jump down? One of the fuel cans must have been holed. The entire cargo bed could go up. He would have to leave Coates. (It might be a kindness.)

The fusillade ceases, a huddled Brinkhurst the first to make himself heard. 'Jesus fell down! Did you hear that? Did you hear the rate of fire?'

'Anybody see him?' asks Swann. 'Somebody must have.'

'Think I saw muzzle flash,' says Mawdsley. 'From that armoured car. Three o'clock.'

The rider cautiously lifts his head to see the wrecked vehicle – broken but not burnt out – positioned a quarter-mile from their right flank. A base for their attacker? Brinkhurst shimmies up to the front of the truck and leans around it to peer through the binoculars. 'Can't see any sign of him. Where in hell is he? Underneath it?' Another burst from the machine gun sends him skidding back behind the wheel arch, fragments of leather and canvas drifting like blossom onto his knees. When the barrage stops again he lifts himself up and slams his palm against the Fordson's cab. 'What's the point, you stupid bastard? We're not fighting any more!' He slumps down again, wearied by his own outrage.

Swann stands on one of the truck's rear tyres and hauls the bundled cache of weapons from the cargo bed. He unties the canvas and lifts out a rifle fitted with a scope, then moves to the front of the vehicle, where he spends a few moments practice-sighting. He concludes with a loud oath and resumes his position of cover, bemoaning the lack of a clear shot, the superior range of the weapon held against them.

And so what now? A gun battle? A prolonged siege? The prospect of either engenders a heavy gloom. What diabolical luck, protests Brinkhurst, that they should be so needlessly delayed. And by their very antithesis, no less, a fellow so intractable in his duty that he will not quit the field, no matter what. The senseless pinnacle of soldierhood.

'We can just take the truck,' says Mawdsley. 'Head that way.' He points westward. 'The Quad will give us cover until we're out of range.'

Brinkhurst shakes his head. He points out a long row of regularly spaced wooden markers, several of them collapsed. Mawdsley swears and drops his head. Impossible to cross a minefield at any reasonable speed.

'Soon fix that,' growls Swann. He scrambles to his feet and edges round the bonnet of the Fordson. He hurriedly unstraps an entrenching tool from its mount on the Quad and returns with it, then beckons Lucchi to dismount from the truck's bed. He performs a brief play of probing the sand, then holds the tool out for the Italian to take. 'Come on then, off you fucken go.' He gestures towards the minefield. 'Chop-chop.'

Lucchi regards the spade with dismay.

'Swann . . .' begins Brinkhurst.

The lance corporal rounds on him. 'You want to do it yourself?'

'He's a prisoner. There are rules.'

'Right. Like the rule you don't shoot down wounded men, the rule that you don't fire on ambulance crews. So how come nobody told *him* the fucken rules?' The lance corporal thrusts the spade into Lucchi's grip, making him flinch.

Brinkhurst absolves himself with raised hands as Swann pushes Lucchi forward, the Italian advancing nervously to the fringes of the mined area to begin broggling around with the metal tip. A murderer then, thinks the rider, of the innocent and wounded. Hard to credit it of him.

Lucchi takes several steps farther, momentarily freezing as the spade brushes a rock. He rubs sweat from his eyes and looks back to Swann, already shaking his head at the tardiness of the operation. The lance corporal appears on the brink of administering some correction when another volley of fire causes everyone to crouch, Lucchi at once fleeing his duty to hurry back to the truck. He throws down the spade and looks to the rider with an expression of beseechment. Why don't you *say* something?

The incensed Swann moves towards him.

'Swann, for God's sake.' Brinkhurst unfurls from his crouch. 'He's too damned jumpy.'

The lance corporal snatches up the spade and slams it against the side of the truck, dismissing the POW with a withering stare. Brinkhurst moves to the Fordson's tailgate, where he takes a moment to survey the intervening terrain. 'What if one of us could get around to the side of him? Maybe keep low behind that ridge and close within rifle range? While we kept him distracted.'

Swann steps over to join him in gauging the distance, the degree of cover. 'Distract him how?'

'We could offer him water,' says Mawdsley. 'Under a flag of

truce. God knows how long he's been there. He has to be thirsty, yes?'

Brinkhurst nods. 'Worth a try.' And then to Swann: 'Don't you think?'

'By "one of us" you mean me, right?' grumbles the lance corporal. 'Seein' as no one else here can shoot worth a shit.'

But there is the question, realises the rider, of who might carry the water. Horribly aware of his own eligibility, he shrinks back in the cargo bed, knowing that there will be no dispensation here, the weakest readily expended, any instinct to charity long since extinguished.

Swann signals to him. 'Umpty. Bring the nearest of those water cans down. Should be half empty.'

Already sickening with dread, the rider drags with him one of the jerrycans marked with a white 'X' as he slides to the tailgate. He hands the can to the lance corporal then clambers weakly from the truck.

'Givin' you the easy job,' mutters Swann. He points over the cargo bed to the bleak tract of sand and rock separating them from their opponent. 'All y'have to do is take this can out to just about where those small boulders are. That should give me enough time to get around to the right of him. Got it?'

The rider struggles for a voice. 'I'm not sure I can.' He looks to the archdeacon. A reprieve on medical grounds? The MO looks away. 'You shouldn't ask me,' he says to Swann. And why? Because it's unfair. No, not unfair, criminal. Criminal and immoral. To send a wounded man. Who would allow such a thing?

'Just pick up the fucken can,' says the lance corporal.

The rider looks with despair to Mawdsley and then to Brinkhurst, both remaining silent. Someone has to do it.

Swann guides him round to the cab of the Quad, then waits until Mawdsley retrieves the white flag from the truck and hoists it on the barrel of a rifle. 'Just keep it steady,' he says, nudging the rider to move out. 'And don't try and fucken look for me. When you hear a shot, hit the dirt. Just in case.'

The rider hesitates, dizzied by fear. *Hold the can up,* somebody hisses. *Show him you're not armed.* Even though it's taking all his strength to remain standing. He wheezes as he lifts his arm, braced already for that nosepoint of lead to drive its way in. What will be worst, the shock or the pain? How many seconds to fully stop a heart?

He steps out into the open, his eyes closed. The air remaining quiet, only the breeze now and then whistling through the ruptured chassis of the Quad. He opens his eyes to the red broth of land. And in the distance the armoured car, a squat beetle, lying in wait.

Still there is no sound from the machine gun, encouraging him to take a tentative step forward. And then another, his raised arm already tiring. He can feel the soreness from his sutured chest, the pain of each insult to muscle and skin revisited. He can sense the eyes of the deserters on his back, the thought overlaying fear with anger. He could spoil the whole enterprise if he chose to. A single quick action, any precipitous move. Almost worth it, if he could muster the courage. But to become some mere refuse beneath the headstone of a water can? Like Coates, he has come too far.

He feels a stab of pain beneath his breastbone, and slowly switches the can to his other hand, lifting it higher then lower, the discomfort varying with each movement. Some vital channel perhaps opened or dammed with each manoeuvre, securing equilibrium.

He continues on, not daring to look anywhere but straight ahead. Where's Swann, the devil take him? Has he reached his position yet? The temptation to glance to his right is furious. Perhaps a glimpse of forearm, the glint of metal passing below the barrier of the ridge. He's at his limit now, a far greater distance than he has yet walked, or could have been expected to walk. How much farther is he supposed to go? He would put the can down now and make his way back but the German might decide he's of no further use and put an end to him. Better to keep going, to keep carrying the water to him. Argue your usefulness.

The shot that rings out pulls him to a startled halt, fearful of the sensation of impact, the dreadful sight of his own blood. And then the realisation that he is not for now the target, that the lance corporal has made his move. Hit the dirt! He drops the can and turns for the safety of the vehicles, anticipating at any moment that vicious storm of metal to follow. The German perhaps bemused at his spasmodic flight, the gracelessness of his stumbling, yard to futile yard. Any second now . . .

When he arrives back at the Quad he is received with surprise by Mawdsley and Brinkhurst, his survival regarded as a curiosity, with only his wretched gulping to refute the supernaturalness of it. 'Holy Christ,' exclaims the ex-captain. 'Swann must have got the bastard.'

But then there is the familiar rasp, like bees in a bell jar, to quell their optimism, sending each man once more plunging for cover. What the hell? Did Swann get him or not? Brinkhurst wipes grit from his forehead, glaring at the rider as though he had practised some deception in returning unscathed.

Swann arrives back shortly after, the lance corporal rising up, grit-lathered, to scuttle back into the cover of the truck. 'Tagged him in the neck,' he announces. 'Three-hundred-yard shot! Goin' to bleed to death for sure, can't be long now.' He looks to the rider with an expression of faint amusement. ''S the matter, Umpty? You didn't trust me?'

Trust. The rider turns away. That the word should even be available to him.

The afternoon burns on without incident, the deserters' anticipation quickly giving way to impatience. At first it's assumed that their assailant must have succumbed, freeing them at last to move on. But what if that's his scheme, playing dead to lure them out? How long does it take a man to drain of blood? Exactly how severe was the wound? Arterial breach, or just a flesh wound? Each impugning of the lance corporal's marksmanship received by him as a personal slight. 'Here's an idea,' he says, presenting

his full height to a leery Brinkhurst. 'Go and finish the fucken job
yourself.'

The ex-captain urges calm, the need for collected thought.
But it's all too much for Swann, who slakes his impulse to action
by turning his attentions instead to the vehicles. Both have been
damaged by bullet impacts, the Quad having sustained punc-
tures to all four of its low-pressure balloon tyres, several strikes
to the engine block confirming its ruin. Two of the Fordson's
tyres have likewise been damaged, and the lance corporal lets air
out of the remaining two to equalise the pressures, allowing the
truck to be drivable for at least the time being. He investigates
the stored cans of petrol to find that three have been holed, a
quantity of fuel having drained into the cargo bed. He decants
any salvaged petrol into the Fordson's tank then sets out two
fuel-soaked blankets and a bedroll to dry. These diversions
exhausted, he takes up the scoped rifle to resume his sniper's station, the endless clicking of the hammer on an empty chamber
driving the others to distraction.

And then there is only the wait, the enduring conflict of prob-
abilities. For a time there remains the suspicion that their gaoler
is simply goading them towards carelessness. But with the passing of the afternoon into early evening, the possibility seems
increasingly remote, leaving only the question of when they
should chance their escape. For Swann each minute is an impo-
sition, the lance corporal careless of risk as he ferries whatever
supplies and equipment are still aboard the Quad to the truck's
dried cargo bed. The task completed, the rest are persuaded to

join him in resuming their travel, each man except for Coates and the rider straining to discern over the grunts and squeals of the overladen truck any sound of a bolt being pulled back, or an ammo belt being slotted into place. Perhaps, thinks the rider, because they envisage a dying man preoccupied entirely with violence, never imagining that he might in the end reject duty and circumstance and reach instead towards home.

He continues to watch as the profile of the armoured car melts into the flatness, the horizon tipping and then levelling as the truck wallows its way from the field.

10

Beastly misfortune. To be delivered into so reprobate a family. Brinkhurst: gentleman inquisitor, bon vivant, liar. Swann: bully, sadist, god to lesser creatures. Mawdsley: curator of analgesics, inductee to that venerable register of opiate-soused, absinthe-swilling quacks. Men of such poor fibre that they find in the openness of the desert only the need to seclude themselves. That they will kill him in the end he has no doubt. Either by calculation or mischance, whichever comes the sooner. A bitter irony after they had themselves rescued him from a certain fate. And a rank injustice, when he has so far weathered every assault against him. A mine inefficiently exploded, a heart scornful of oxygen, the bullets of an aeroplane cannon drawn wayward in ballistic anomaly: certainly a more tenacious survivor than any might think possible, even when smiled upon by chance. And perhaps such good fortune might continue if he could only slip his uncaring bed-fellows. But how to engineer the break, there's the dilemma ...

Coates disturbs him by kicking his shin, the Canadian once again fallen to a half-sleep, his crumpled form bounced and rocked by the jolting of the truck. The night has brought a biting cold, all four men in the cargo bed wrapped in blankets and coats, the canvas re-secured over the hoops to afford some extra insulation. The rider lifts a corner of the unstrapped rear flap to see a thin tunnel of dust raised in their wake, the outlying plains an unbroken shingle of ores and minerals, aglow under an alien moon. It would be quicker for them to make their way across such flatter terrain, but they are tacking instead to a course of heavier sand, where there is less risk to the deflating tyres.

The Fordson slows, and he turns to look in the direction of their travel. A quarter of a mile ahead and east of their trajectory there is a wave of pale rock prised upward, a large vehicle lodged dark as an arrowhead into its flank. After a brief conference with Brinkhurst, Swann steers the truck in the direction of the ridge and picks up their speed again, the detail of the vehicle becoming clear as they close in. An Allied tank, the steel plate of its hull flowered inward, exposing the pale turret basket inside.

Swann stops the truck's engine at the scene and he and Brinkhurst dismount, both men taking a moment to study the tank's unfamiliar contours and dimensions, its multiple tiers suggesting the wall-works and ramparts of a medieval fort, its heavy main gun displaced to one side and housed in the fashion of a destroyer's battery.

'Brute of a thing,' says the ex-captain. 'Seen one of these before, Swann?'

The lance corporal shakes his head. He collects a flashlight from the truck's cab and shines it over the ground in front of the tank, checking for the telltale prongs of a bouncing *Schrapnellmine* or the pancaked depression of a Teller. He angles the beam into the hull's torn cavity, scanning for any wires or charges, then cautiously pokes his head inside. He pulls back and drags a finger across his throat. No survivors.

'Anything we can use?' enquires Brinkhurst.

The lance corporal performs a quick walk-round of the exterior. 'Bolt cutter, engine crank. Spade, tow cable, track adjuster. Nothin' much.' He nods towards the tank's interior. 'She must have driven out here off the hand throttle, stalled against the rock.' He bends to examine the right-side track, moving the palm of his hand along the heads of the pins. He inspects the drive sprocket and bogie assemblies before moving to the tank's left side to do the same. 'Tracks and running gear still OK.'

'Could we siphon the petrol?'

The lance corporal unlatches one of the outer stowage lockers to pull out a small selection of food tins. 'What's the point? Truck's done. Can't be more than half a day's travel left in her.'

The rider studies the tank with fascination. Something in its angles and parabolae, its elevations and projections. He shifts his gaze to the deep tear in the hull. The shock of impact, that paralysing moment of terror. Who having survived such a trial could forget it?

He feels a nudge against his ankle and sees that Coates has stirred at the commotion. The spit hawker takes up the grease pencil to scrawl on his board, and the rider drags aside the canvas to allow him more light.

ASK HOW FAR TO CAIRO

'I'll find out,' the rider promises.

Brinkhurst appears in the triangle of opened canvas. He takes a moment to read Coates' message. 'We'll be stopping here for a bit. Get a brew on, grab some kip. Push on in the morning.' And to Coates: 'We're making good progress, don't worry.' He beckons for Mawdsley to dismount and join him.

The rider looks at the nervous Lucchi and makes the motion of lifting a mug to his lips. The Italian smiles and helps the rider shuffle Coates to the tailgate, both men helping him slide from the bed. The Canadian barely has time to orient himself before all are drawn to the spectacle of a distant skyburst to the north-east, a canopy of incandescence briefly hanging. A second flare shoots upward, prompting a short expletive from Brinkhurst. He looks to Swann, still gazing in the direction of the signals. 'How far do you reckon?'

'Five, six miles maybe.'

'Probably moving north. Best to let them pull some ground on us.'

With a burst of will, Coates breaks from the rider's grip and topples against the truck's tailgate, the writing plate already lifted to his chest.

GET HELP

And then ...

MORPHINE

Brinkhurst steps forward. 'All right, now come on, Coates. Think straight. We don't even know who it is out there.'

DONT CARE
WANT HOSPITAL
~~Ba~~ PLEASE!

The rider catches Coates as he slumps again, the tin falling from his grip. 'We could just take him part of the way? Turn him loose?'

Brinkhurst nods impatiently. 'And what do you think happens when they find him? *If* they find him.'

Coates makes a wild flailing motion, knocking a tube from his throat, and Mawdsley hurries to attend to him. The spit hawker makes a series of groans, each punctuated by a bubbling stop. Wails of frustration? Speech? Brinkhurst gives a sad shake of his head. 'Hardly doing himself any good ...'

The rider and Lucchi guide Coates away, the Italian fetching a bedroll so that they can prop him against the barrier of stone. The rider pulls up the collar of the Canadian's greatcoat but notices he's no longer shivering, despite the cold. He delves into the pockets of the coat to find the familiar pack of cards. Pinochle? Gin rummy? Two-player whist? The spit hawker regards him briefly as if to say, Thank you, but no.

The rider looks back to the truck, where Swann has already lit a petrol burner on which to boil water, Brinkhurst doling out hard-tack biscuits between them. The familiar sordid council. He returns his attention to Coates, who is reaching into a shirt pocket. The Canadian lifts out his crumpled wedding photograph and puts it into the rider's hand, then fumbles for his writing board and grease pencil.

DONT TELL ABOUT FACE

The rider nods. He's not sure what to do with the photograph but takes it nonetheless, Coates afterwards closing his eyes to settle back against the rock. The rider murmurs a parting reassurance then rises to walk over to the deserters, who appear surprised at his intrusion, their conversation withering in his presence.

'Can I talk to you in private?' he says to Brinkhurst.

'If you must.' The ex-captain makes a gesture of apology to the others. He leads the rider away, drawing them both to a stop once they are beyond earshot. 'I'm afraid I shan't change my mind about Coates.'

'I think I should leave.'

Brinkhurst sips at his tea. 'You do?'

'I'm a burden to you.'

'Yes, you are. How will you travel, have you thought?'

'I'll walk.'

'You'll walk. In your condition. And how far do you think you'd get? Where would you go?'

'I'll head east, towards British lines.'

'Or German. You could be stuck in a camp for years. If they don't shoot you on the spot, that is.'

'It's my risk.'

'Actually it's our risk. That you might get caught, that you might start blabbing your mouth off. This isn't some garden party you can politely retire from.'

'I wouldn't talk.'

'Because you're trained not to, is that it? The man who won't break? Because forgive me, but you don't strike me as that kind of fellow at all.'

The rider shivers, suddenly exhausted.

Brinkhurst looks towards the truck and lowers his voice. 'Look, I'm sorry you were given that job with the water. It wouldn't have been my choice, you know that. It's Swann. If we didn't need him so much ...'

The rider nods. The ex-captain as cozener again.

'But what's important is for us to stick together. At least for now. I might not like it any better than you, but it's the practical thing to do. You can see that, surely?' He flings the rest of the tea from the mug and watches it drain. 'So why don't you just hang in there with us for the time being? Once we're in the Green

Mountain you can decide for yourself. That's reasonable, don't you think?' He pulls a packet of cigarettes from his coat pocket. 'So I gather you must be feeling a little better then. More yourself?'

The rider looks away. Give him nothing.

'Well, there you are then.' Brinkhurst lights a cigarette and discards the match. 'Just try to think clearly. That's all. Try and consider the bigger picture. You can do that, can't you?' He gives the rider an amiable clap on the shoulder and walks back to the others, hand cupped over the burning tip.

Returned to his station, the rider tries unsuccessfully for sleep, his attention shifting every now and then to the nearby Coates, who must remain upright, a backwash of vomit and other humours of decay still threatening. Sometimes he will list precariously, as though discreetly assassinated, causing the rider to flush with panic and then indecision. The greater mercy perhaps being to allow him to drown. But then the spit hawker will right himself, the instinct of balance uncannily restored, lifting the weight of responsibility.

After each of these alarms the rider is left further unsettled, his gaze turning to a ceiling of starpoints, among which he is able to spy from time to time a dark nebula of gravel and shale. And across it a legion of armoured vehicles attended by fitters, engineers and welders, the brilliance from their blowtorches describing a spare galaxy. If he closes his eyes he finds himself able to travel closer still to see crewmen gathered to their vehicles, each fellow huddled in a greatcoat or blanket to a petrol-burning stove. BIG SIS they have daubed on their tank. Or MISS MISERY or TIMBUKTU OR BUST or DEVIL MAY CARE. These spirited christenings at odds with the uncertainty behind their eyes or the tremor at their knuckles, each of them alert to those dread rumours that burn like slow fuses between them.

But then teams of mechanics will erect tarpaulin bowers to mask any clues of light, and the entire assembly will be eclipsed beneath a mezzanine of hide, leaving the rider excluded. The veil at length pulled clear to reveal a surface scored with directionless trackmarks and debossed with a frenzy of bootprints, as though all present might at once have been released by gravity and swept off.

No way for him to follow, even if he wanted.

At first light he finds Coates barely breathing, the uncovered part of his face pale as bone. He elects not to disturb him, deciding instead to refill the canteens, and makes his way over to the truck to find Brinkhurst and Swann beneath the shelter of a bivouac, both men poring over a map.

'Change of plan?'

Brinkhurst looks up at him. 'Swann has some experience driving Yank Honeys onto rail cars. He says this one is quite similar . . .'

'It's called a Grant,' says the rider. 'After the General.'

The ex-captain frowns.

'I remember the name. That's all.'

Brinkhurst glances to the lance corporal before continuing. 'Swann checked the gauges this morning. There's enough fuel left to get us another fifty miles or so. The batteries are low but they'll charge on the move.'

'What about the truck?'

'Forget the truck,' grumbles Swann. 'Couple of shot tyres, an oil leak and a rad that's pissin' out coolant.'

Brinkhurst says, 'We'll switch everything we can to the tank once we know we can get it started. You feel up to giving a hand?'

'I was bringing Coates some water.'

'Mawdsley can see to that. Just leave the canteens.'

Swann grabs a can of paraffin and a folded shirt from the Fordson's cargo bed. He tears up the shirt and hands several pieces to the rider as he leads him to the tank. He hoists himself through the side hatch and proceeds to open the driver's view port and roof hatch while the rider takes a moment to reappraise the vehicle, nervous at the prospect of recollection. He slides his hands across the curve of the transmission cover, the solid plate of the glacis, finding at once a familiarity in their Braille of rivets. Such things perhaps residing as a deeper awareness, an innateness of self. The body learning what the mind refuses?

'Couple in here and another two in the turret,' calls Swann. 'We'll get these two out first. Grab ahold when I drag 'em over to you. Stop if I shout.'

The rider hears him grunting and cursing inside the crew

compartment. Finally the lance corporal hauls the first pair of shoulders to the hatch, the man's neck capped by an ugly twist of bone and scalp. The rider looks away as he pulls, the hips and thighs sliding out like a landed fish. He waits for the next body and drags it clear, Swann afterwards reappearing at the hatch, cheek smeared with blood. He clambers out and wipes his hands. 'Goin' to drag the other two out from the top. You can finish up in here. Sticks and pedals need a wipe-down, same for the breech.' He climbs to the tank's upper deck, where he begins heaving at the bodies folded into the turret.

The rider squeezes gingerly into the side hatch, a paraffin-soaked rag in his hand. He manoeuvres himself forward to sit in the driver's seat then turns to look at the main gun's breech, its recoil guard, its elevation and traverse wheels. This view that ought to be scored somehow into the back of his skull. Yet still nothing to elicit the reawakening he had expected. Not even the collection of scents – cordite, baked rubber, urine, scorched lead paint – stirring any recall.

Disappointed, he gives the control levers and instrument panel a quick wipe-down and climbs from the tank, Swann meanwhile hauling the bodies of the crewmen over to a dumping spot beneath the wave of rock. No one caring to argue for a more careful burial, the sand in any case recognised as the final agent of interment. The lance corporal swabs his face and hands with paraffin and re-enters the crew compartment, his efforts at the controls rewarded with a dull shudder from the motor. He disembarks again and proceeds to the rear of the tank, where he unclips a starter tool from its deck mounts. He cranks the engine a dozen times then returns to the driver's seat, the tank again rumbling briefly before choking. After a moment he emerges from the cabin, pulls down his mask and wipes the sweat from his eyes. 'Piece of shit won't start.'

He ponders a moment and then strides over to Brinkhurst, now occupied with the business of stocktaking. 'She won't fire off the batteries. Plugs could be fouled, I'll give 'em a look. There's a Homelite on board, so maybe I can juice up the batteries from that. Once she gets going we'll need to push off, make best use of the fuel.'

'How sure are you that it'll start?'

'I'll get her running, all right. Just get everythin' ready for the switch.'

He returns to the tank's engine bay, toolkit in hand, the rider watching as he unscrews and removes several spark plugs, wiping each clean of oil before replacing them.

'What can I do to help?' he asks.

The lance corporal rises to his knees, faintly surprised, his chin and brow black with oil. 'We need to try the generator. You could keep an eye on the gauges.'

'I can do that.'

Swann leads him back to the crew compartment, both men climbing inside one after the other. The lance corporal squeezes himself close to the hull-mounted generator and uses a screwdriver to prise off the circular magneto shield. He winds the pull cord onto the rim of the starter plate and gives it a sharp tug to fire up the generator's motor, then pushes the battery button on the control box. He indicates for the rider to seat himself in the driver's position and bends over his shoulder to point to the ammeter and voltmeter gauges. 'Let me know when those needles budge.' He moves to leave the compartment then pauses. 'You should probably know. We won't be takin' Coates. Poor bastard's done.' He hauls himself back out of the hatch and into daylight.

The rider remains still, watching the needles as they begin their slow dance between latency and life. So there it is, the spit hawker's fate coldly laid out. There'll be no rescue for him, no delivery. He must suffer the process to its end. A good man might insist on staying with him. A kind man might do that. But would it be the right thing? What if he could find no help? What if the Germans simply shot him down, as Brinkhurst had suggested? Perhaps it's too soon to strike out on his own.

The needles begin to judder then steadily turn, and he shouts for Swann, who quickly arrives to look over the dials. He takes the rider's place in the driver's seat and thumbs the fuel primer, then flicks the booster button and start switches. On the second attempt the tank's engine starts with a bang, the entire vehicle trembling at the report before settling to a steady rhythm. 'You beauty,' he shouts, slapping the instrument panel. He declutches and engages reverse gear, giving the tank enough throttle for it to back slowly away from the rock face, its retreat heralded by a groan of metal. He puts it into park and abandons his seat, leaving the engine running. 'Bloody Yanks for you,' he shouts. 'Better late than never.'

Both men exit the tank, Swann urging speed in transferring their thinned-down supplies. Excused from the most arduous work, the rider sifts through the supplies and materiel that cannot now be accommodated, selecting some of the equipment to leave with Coates. A spare bedroll, an empty kitbag to use as a pillow. When the others finally gather to the Canadian for their farewell, only a few words of polite sympathy are offered, all privately relieved that he now lacks the perception to understand. Mawdsley suggests that they lay the red cross flag as a marker for his location, and the sheet is duly draped. There is the unspoken feeling that something more should be done or said, but time is pressing and precious fuel going to waste.

Brinkhurst takes up position in the Grant's turret while the rider and Lucchi seat themselves on its upper deck, Mawdsley squeezing into the crew compartment along with the caged chickens. Swann resumes his driver's seat and guides the tank via a number of brake turns from their enclave and out onto open ground, the squeal and clatter of its track plates matching the din from its engine.

For the first few minutes of their journey the rider looks back to the painted sheet, vivid now under the morning sun. There will be one final awakening for the spit hawker, he decides. One of no purpose but to show him a shifting world, his limbs effaced, the flag of his burial covered over. He might wonder at the horizon of hourglasses, at the circus of vultures. If he could speak a final word it would be his wife's name. When he succumbs he will stay reposed as one living until the winds topple him, then go undiscovered. Scout cars will rove within a mile of him, their drivers seeing only bare country, itinerant Bedouin hearing no rumour of him. Other names will pass into the desert and be given up to conjecture before his own. He will become at length a mere artefact, the trappings of soldiery girded about him like paraphernalia of the old kings.

And if he is ever found, then they will dismiss without care what remains of him, speculating only briefly on how such a fellow might have come to lose his face.

11

The Grant continues on to an empty expanse, all flourishes of land ceded now to a featureless divide between earth and sky. If any vessels were to appear on the horizon they might describe in their travel the circumferential arc, a sight familiar to mariners but still astonishing to land dwellers. Across the breadth of the vista, the air lifts and rolls in apparitional breakers, conjuring visions of mythic skylines, the canopies of secret waterholes. And for the rider, one illusion to supersede all others: that grand temple in which he had earlier trespassed, revealed to him now in a flourish of baking air. And why? The soul seeking redemption? The gateway to an absolution?

Except that if he gives himself to that imagining he finds only the promise of a greater struggle, wooden gantries now leaned up into the heights of the dome, every degree of its orbit panelled with shelving, gridded with book spines. Because here, he realises, you must strive for enlightenment, you must *achieve* it, hauling yourself like the cathedral builders of old to the magisterial apex, to apotheosis.

He sees that none of the others is watching, each of them mesmerised by the same infinity. No one to take notice as he begins his private escalade, the height becoming dizzying as he ascends hand over hand into a great dance of dust, motes of parchment and vellum caught in the crossbeams. A short ladder leading finally to a study room spaced with reading tables, heavy with the perfumes of ink, floor wax and old leather.

'Stay sharp now,' snaps Brinkhurst. 'Eyes front. Keep your focus.'

'I'll try,' mumbles the rider.

The tank motors on across the flat, the land marked here and there by weals in the crust above which turbulent air musters. The ground otherwise so insistently regular that the same expanse seems to repeat itself over and again, nature having lost its will to miscellany. The magnetic compass is no longer working, Brinkhurst announces, suggesting that they are driving across a vast sheet of iron. The sun compass likewise useless, thanks to a meridian sun. So they must try to travel directly forward to be sure of their course, each man hoping that the air might remain clear, aware that if a sandstorm were to come upon them now they would surely be lost, doomed to roam the multiplying sameness until reduced to a conglomerate of rust and bones.

They emerge at last from the baking sea onto more varied terrain, the ground now interrupted by roots of stone which sporadically wind upward into inverted pots and basins, each grooved as though turned on a wheel. The appearance of a more knowable land encourages a better humour in all, and even Swann allows himself the mischief of now and then yanking on the brakes, dislodging Brinkhurst from his turret perch and threatening to fling each man from the deck like loads from a ballista. Each time the irate ex-captain fumbling with the intercom to issue such unorthodox commands as, 'Steady on there, Swann', and 'A little more finesse, if you please, Swann'.

After several more miles they encounter the site of a Muslim shrine, a cube of white stone topped by a sagging clay dome. And an old cemetery set out beside it, each of the grave markers collapsed into rubble. At first they look at the building with some wariness, thinking it perhaps the den for another marooned assailant. But it appears to be empty, not even any sign of a nearby settlement to populate the graves, leading them finally to view it with the same dull curiosity as any other desert wonder as the tank rumbles past.

The rider looks back to the shrine as they open a distance upon it, the shape of it now fluid in the haze. If he gazes long enough he can pick out stained-glass windows, stone buttresses, oaken doors. A country church perhaps, its grounds thronged with wedding guests, the crowd parting to make way for her as she passes.

Her oil-sodden work clothes put away now in favour of gown and veil, her arm entwined with that of her new husband, immaculate in his dress uniform. Except that if he looks more keenly he can see that he shares no similarity of feature with the groom. A younger fellow than himself, more fresh-faced and darker-haired. Second Lieutenant James Tuck, no doubt, arrived to ruin his most delicate of designs. What spite!

He looks and looks again, the entire scene tumbling into dust. Fool, to presume certainty in so nascent a universe, all acts of creation probationary. An anecdote passed between friends haphazardly built upon, a wish fulfilled by proxy. All these stories and names ventured into, turned now to traps.

He leans wearily against the deck as they continue on their assumed northerly bearing, the ground becoming a greater test with each mile covered, scrub-spotted hummocks swelling like cankers through the surface, deep gullies running between them. Sometimes the channels are wide enough to navigate through, other times the tank cresting and diving like a liner on a bow wave as it fords the divides. Brinkhurst does his best to guide Swann over the crossings but occasionally the incline will give way, or they will misjudge a distance, causing the Grant to skew violently left or right, its passengers grappling for some handhold to stop themselves skidding from the deck. They really must take care, cautions Brinkhurst. Continue like this and they might throw a track, become beached on some stubborn atoll, installing themselves as a monument to imprudence. Too near the prize to be defeated now.

All are relieved when the undulations lead finally onto a craquelured tabletop of stone, allowing the tank more reliably to bridge the faults. Some of the breaches widening as they push on, others splaying into a delta of tributaries. The same anatomy, broods the rider, as a dead lung, inert air collecting in each filamental path. How much farther? It's becoming harder for him to stay awake, more difficult to find focus. The midday heat absorbed and radiated by the tank's steel plate, the smells of burning grease and exhaust fumes overpowering. Only the vehicle's jarring and shuddering preventing him from succumbing to his drowsiness and slipping into the rising clouds.

He is restored to alertness by Lucchi, who turns from his outboard seat to call out, his finger pointed northward to several sprites of dust tracking in a straight line above the surface. And beyond it, at farther range, a tall ridge spanning the horizon, like some fabled city wall of antiquity. Brinkhurst lifts his binoculars then calls over the intercom for Swann to halt the tank while he consults his maps. That's it, he declares, the Akhdar range. The end of the desert! It seems barely conceivable that such overwhelming immensity might have its limits, each man moved almost to euphoria at the prospect of it. But there's an obstacle, warns Brinkhurst. This is the first of two roads they must cross, both of them metalled highways – approximately five miles apart – which function as the main arteries for military resupply. There's some traffic on the first, several soft-skinned vehicles heading east. Almost certainly enemy, he qualifies, to judge by their direction. They'll need to wait a little, make sure the vehicles aren't part of some convoy.

For most, the stoppage comes as a welcome break, each man taking the opportunity to disembark and stretch his legs, both the rider and Lucchi beating dust from their hair and clothing. The Italian thinks to lift the chicken cage from the stifling crew compartment and place it in the only area of shade beneath the belly of the tank. He begins to slide under the hull to join them when he is apprehended by Swann, the lance corporal shirtless and sheened with sweat, a strip of cloth tied as a headband. He unlatches one of the stowage bins to retrieve a grease can and rag. 'Clean the wheels,' he orders. 'Then grease them. Like this. See?' He wipes one of the bogie wheels and then applies grease from the can's applicator nozzle before planting both can and rag against Lucchi's chest. 'All of them. Don't miss any.'

Lucchi stands in bewilderment, a trail of dried spittle parting the sand on his chin. '*Molto stanco*,' he whispers. So tired . . .

Swann's threat of a cuff makes him cower. 'Just fucken do it.'

The rider exchanges glances with Brinkhurst, who quickly returns to his map. It's a necessary job, after all. Swann uncorks his canteen and spreads a little water over his lips before taking a short swig. He notices the rider's gaze upon him and spits a wad of saliva, then proceeds to the front of the tank, his eye on the distant road.

The archdeacon comes to stand nearby, watching as Lucchi struggles with his task. He pulls a matchbox from his shorts pocket and shakes from it a small pill. 'Best to keep out of it,' he says. 'Believe me.' He slips one of the pills into his mouth.

The rider holds him in a stare. 'You said my lungs couldn't heal. A matter of weeks, you said.'

'I said it was hard to predict. You're doing well. Better than expected. Be glad of it.'

'And now?'

'We might hope for more. Some recall, perhaps.' He waits, as though for confirmation. 'Then you'll have to decide what you want to tell us.'

The rider hesitates. 'You're suggesting I have something to hide?'

'Beyond the fact of you being here with us? Not necessarily.'

Discomfited, the rider points to his shin. 'I wanted to ask you about this mark on my leg. It looks like a burn. But not a recent one.'

The archdeacon smiles, the starfishes of broiled skin crumpling. 'That's the thing about burns. They never heal. The skin simply hardens. Nothing helps.'

'If I could remember the cause of it . . .'

'It's a frustration, I'm sure. But you'll arrive at some explanation. You'll keep us apprised?'

He signals his leaving with a quick nod and turns to walk back towards Brinkhurst. Just as expected of him: those beneficent palms empty, nothing but the usual sham. And perhaps inevitably so in this realm of cheats and fantasists, where a man might become victim even to his own mistruths. An invented sweetheart, an assumed lieutenancy, the thrill of confabulation obscuring rationality. A more exacting approach is required.

He collects his postbag from the tank and takes himself to the front of the Grant, its transmission cover providing a thin rectangle of shade. He pulls out the envelopes and sifts through them, the names now beginning to assume a greater familiarity. The beginnings of recollection? Or simply the consequence of repetition?

Perhaps this time he should look more closely to those men carrying no duties of leadership. The instinct for command surely ingrained as a second nature, not so easily slid away with a shelf of grey matter. What officer after all would submit so readily to such shirkers and apostates as these? Better to look for himself among the ordinary, to presume anonymity.

One must be grateful at least . . .

Writes Trooper Oxburgh,

. . . for that comradeship with one's fellows, which has made
even the hardest things easier. Despite all we have been through,
not a one of us here has been lonely, every hope and fear shared.
Sometimes I wonder if we are not all the same man, separated
only by manner and habit. Would it offend against Christian
thought, do you think, to suppose such a thing?

But it's becoming hard to think through it, every thread lost to the scorching updraft. He tries again.

Trooper Jack Warren:

... but I know you will understand, my darling, when I say
that I have longed for those rare times when I could be alone.
We are all deep in each other's business here, with few secrets
between us, and there have been no more treasured moments for
me than those spent in the quiet hold of a ship, or in the
emptiness of our leaguered tank, when I could make my escape
back to you.

It's too hot, too dry. He drops the letter to shimmy beneath the tank, relieved to have darkness across his face, grateful for cooler air. And a more miraculous escape still if he closes his eyes: to a chamber hollowed from stone and shin-deep in water, a bolus of light at his feet, pale spinnakers coasting the walls. The hall of some ancient aquifer, aeons of rainwater drained through the limestone. They're waiting for him, calling him from above, man after man peering through the sinkhole to look for him in the shadows. Each face indistinguishable from the next. Time to move on! Ready to go! Give me a moment, he hears himself call. Wishing at the same time that a moment might be an hour, and that hour a day and that day a month, so that his absence might at last be given up to mystery, allowing him to emerge unnoticed, superfluous to the engine of war.

Give me a moment. Did he say the words, or just think them?

A boot strikes hard against his ankle, fetching him from his shelter. Fuck's sake, Umpty.

Not much time, elaborates Brinkhurst. The road appears clear, their opportunity arrived. They need to take their chance.

Swann snatches the greasing tool back from Lucchi and hurriedly stows it before climbing back through the side hatch, the others still clambering back into position as the engine fires. Within minutes the tank is again mobile, Lucchi and the rider resuming their positions on deck, the former with the chicken cage in his arms. Like some rustic chased cruelly from his patch, thinks the rider, hugging close the dearest of his possessions.

They push as hard as they dare over the several miles to the road, Swann urging the tank to its best speed, a tall bloom of dust lifting about them as they bounce towards their destination. No highway that civilisation would recognise, but a more rudimentary construct, sand shuffled over its entire breadth, its surface cracked and blistered by the weight of armoured vehicles, and cratered here and there by explosive impact. A marvel nonetheless against these trackless outlands.

Their final approach appears at first to have been timed well, the road clear in both directions. Then the rider sees a distant funnel of dust, from something small and fast-moving. A jeep perhaps, or lightweight truck. He squints harder and turns to alert Brinkhurst, but the ex-captain has already seen it, the binoculars tight against his face.

'Bloody straggler,' he says grimly. 'Looks like an armoured car.'

What to do? Halt, or make the crossing? The Grant doubtless already sighted. If they continue on the car might give chase, opening fire on the tank's hindquarters, on the engine compartment, the fuel tanks. Brinkhurst gives the command to halt, the Grant lurching to a stop some fifty yards shy of the road's raised verges. He ducks down and yells for Mawdsley to man the turret gun, the MO just as quickly pointing out that he has no idea how to operate it. But of course, why would he? No drills, no training, no thought of anything except to put themselves as far as possible from harm's way. Swann shouts his intention to take his place, but Brinkhurst is quick to gainsay. The lance corporal needs to stay where he is, they may need to drive out of this. And then it's all too late anyway, the armoured car slowing along the highway until it comes to a stop at right angles to them, the flak cannon of its open-top turret aimed squarely at the rider and live-stock-burdened Lucchi.

'Steady,' murmurs Brinkhurst, slipping into the cupola. 'Steady now . . .'

The rider notices the barrel of the Grant's turret machine gun jolt and then lower. What to do? Jump down? Or might that initiate battle? Lucchi looks to him with frightened eyes, as though he might offer some direction. Swann's growl audible from the gunner's hatch. 'Come on then, you bastards. What's it to be?'

The grilles over the armoured car's turret flip open, provoking a further wave of alarm. A stocky fellow in service cap and white scarf emerging, his shirt open to the waist. He raises his hands before jumping from the car, then walks towards the Grant until no more than twenty feet distant, at which point he stops and points towards the caged chickens.

'Wie viel kosten die Hühner?'

He looks to the rider and Lucchi, both of them dumbfounded. Brinkhurst raises himself cautiously from the cupola, just as incredulous. 'No sale,' he calls back, sweeping his hands back and forth. 'You can't buy.'

The German makes a sour face. '*Na gut, haben Sie Eier?*' He sketches an oval shape in the air. '*Können Sie uns Eier verkaufen?*'

Brinkhurst leans down into the turret to hiss, 'Mawdsley, how many bloody eggs do we have?' He straightens himself again. 'Three. *Drei.* You can have three eggs. No charge!'

The German waits patiently while Mawdsley is despatched with the eggs, then inspects them carefully on receipt. Satisfied, he nods towards Brinkhurst then takes a further moment to study the lines of the Grant. '*Amerikanisch?*' he asks Mawdsley.

The MO says yes, prompting a shake of the head from the German before he turns and trudges back to the armoured car. He glances one more time at the tank before closing the turret grilles, the vehicle then pulling sedately away, gaining distance until it is no more than an accent in the haze.

The deserters remain momentarily in position, no one willing to make any comment on the episode. Only when they are quite certain that they will now be unimpeded do they resume their travel, the tank rolling over the flat causeway and down onto a series of low ridges before motoring away across the sand field beyond.

12

Shit! says Swann. Shit, shit and a thousand times shit! An offence perhaps to his wrangler's pride that he is unable to explain the Grant's sudden stoppage. Could it be the batteries? The fuel? The gauges show plenty. Then what?

Who knows. Simply some twist of fortune for which there is no explanation and for which he certainly can't be held accountable. The worst of it is that they're so close now, perhaps only five or six miles from safety. Bloody galling, admits Brinkhurst, but there it is. At least the last of the roads is behind them, only empty ground ahead. All the same, there's no sense in making camp here in this wide-open sand field, a prize to any half-blinkered spotter. They can walk the remainder. It won't kill them.

The ex-captain takes the lack of argument as his signal to initiate the disembarkation, assigning Mawdsley, Lucchi and the rider to remove from the tank whatever they might carry in the way of supplies. They'll need to take what food they can pack into kitbags, fill their water bottles, gather any spare clothing and bedding and divide the weapons cache, each man bearing whatever weight of arms he can shoulder. There are the chickens too, Lucchi standing over the cage in enquiry. '*Che cosa facciamo?*'

'The meat will stay fresh for a few hours,' suggests Mawdsley.

Brinkhurst looks to Lucchi and makes a chopping action with his palm. The Italian stares at him and then shakes his head. He lifts the cage and bounces it in his arms to show that the weight is bearable.

'You can't carry it, you silly bastard. It's too far. Big long way. *Capisci?*' Brinkhurst looks to Swann, now leaning against the stalled Grant, water bottle in his hand. 'Swann, tell him.'

The lance corporal takes a swig from the canteen and watches as Lucchi collects a piece of frayed webbing from a pile of clothing and weaves it around the frame of the chicken cage. The POW pulls the ends of the webbing over his shoulders and hoists the cage onto his back.

Swann shrugs. 'Up to him.'

'But it's pointless. There are better things for him to carry.'

'Right. Like your tinker's stash? Is that it?'

'Those are things we can use for barter. Come on, that's how we do this. We deal, we exchange, we buy our way through. You've seen it! Look, it's not my fault the bloody tank stopped. What do you want me to do?'

'Do what you want. It's your stuff.'

Brinkhurst glares at him and then breaks from the stand-off, jaw muscle vainly at work. He looks to Mawdsley and then to the rider. Then, red-faced, he drags his case of baggage onto the dry soil and opens it. So which is it to be? A bottle of Chianti or a gilded clock? A ceremonial dagger or an Italian medal? Flustered by the others' impatience, he wraps any items vulnerable to damage in fabrics before stuffing the final complement of booty into a KD haversack. He clears his forehead with his shirtsleeve and pulls the haversack onto his back, then falls in line as Swann leads the group off, Bren gun over his shoulder, the Grant left as a stripped-down curio, plain for any to see.

Though the rider has only his postbag, a haversack of tins, a bedroll and several bundled tools to carry, he still finds it impossible to keep up. His thigh and calf muscles periodically seizing, his breathing reduced to a pitiful wheeze, every trudging step accompanied by thoughts of an imminent doom. Not that they'll care of course, his fellow absconders. As long as he's able to haul his load some of the way, he'll have proved to be of use. His ultimate worth – as expected – measured out in feet and yards.

And then disaster, quite devastating in its suddenness. An immediate and complete draining of himself, all animatory forces revoked. No pain this time, but rather a cataclysmic loss of energy that drops him to his knees, his hands fluttering at once to his ribs, as though there might be some breaker there to restore the current. It was bound to happen; he's been pushing himself far too hard. The clubs of chest pain, the light-headedness, the episodes of hallucination: all warning signs. And now not even the strength to raise himself up. Bitter fortune!

Brinkhurst is the first to notice, the ex-captain turning to see him crumpled, a milestone as pitiable as the dead Frenchman they had encountered. A longitude of defeated souls continued.

Hands on hips, the ex-captain looks up to a dulling sky and then down to his feet. Horribly tiresome, but he'll have to backtrack.

He makes the distance at the double and comes to rest, politely out of breath, on one knee. Then asks idiotically: 'What's the matter?'

'I can't do it. I can't make it.'

'Giving up, then. Throwing in the towel. Can't say I'm surprised. But you should know you're letting yourself down. Yourself and us. You do know that? We'll have to leave some of the equipment behind. Because you've decided you want to jack it in.'

The rider gazes through medically explicable tears. 'You don't know what I've done.'

Brinkhurst glances to Swann, now towering at his shoulder. Then back to the rider. 'What do you mean? What have you done?'

The rider drops his head. 'I don't know.'

Brinkhurst makes a clucking noise and stands. 'It's the heat. Dehydration, or something. Damned nuisance.'

The archdeacon is summoned, but a quick examination offers no surprises. Damaged lungs, a failing heart, what can one expect? Brinkhurst pulls his revolver and pauses to wipe a spot of grease from the grip. 'You know what I'm going to ask,' he says to the rider.

Yes, I know.

'Quicker than you just lying here. Just waiting. So there's the choice. If your mind's made up, that is.'

Swann steps forward. 'No sense wastin' a bullet.' He begins to lift the straps from the rider's shoulders. 'Sun'll do for him. Or the cold. One or the other. 'S what he wants, anyway.'

The rider is tugged forward as Swann pulls away his canteen. Such easy cruelty. A dispassion to match that of the desert itself. He clings to the strap of his postbag.

Brinkhurst holsters his revolver, satisfied after a quick three-sixty of the surrounding terrain that the scene will not be chanced upon. 'I don't know what it is with you,' he says. 'Always looking for sympathy. Always a show. Perhaps it's attention you want. Anyway. There's no point wishing you luck. You won't be found. Not here. Not ever, I shouldn't think.'

The rider watches them resume their march, Lucchi taking a moment to signal a wan farewell before wading away with the others. Four dissolutes inked out in red; it's all part of the new spectrum. He looks down to his postbag. *A great thing you did.* Except you hadn't passed on those precious testimonials, but kept them to yourself. Because you want them lost, buried? No greater resolution but this?

He tests himself again, stretching his arms out, flexing his calf and thigh muscles, his control over them temporarily restored. And his breathing? Steady again, for the moment.

He raises himself to his knees and then to his feet, relocating his balance with each step. None of the criminals ahead even sparing a backward glance, as though his death was already a matter of record.

He continues to track them nonetheless, his gaze firmly on Brinkhurst's dwindling frame. Just a little empathy from him, some small encouragement, that was all he'd needed. But then of course the ex-captain would be a nobler soul, and would never have been with them in the first place.

Even so, it's tempting to believe that he might still – somehow – break from that inflexible mould to display a more benevolent nature. Possible even to imagine that more compassionate rendition of him falling back in comradeship, as convincing in form and detail as any trick of the desert:

A Kinder Brinkhurst

Thought I'd tag along for a bit. That's if you don't mind? Give you a little company. I know I've been remiss on that side of things. No excuse for it really, but there it is. Better late than never.

Anyway, I've been speaking to Mawdsley, and he thinks you're doing quite marvellously. In fact we all do. That you should pull yourself together like this and push on – it's the stuff of real grit, and no mistake.

And you should know that if things come to the worst and you don't make it, then we'll certainly give you a proper and decent send-off.

In fact, I can tell you that when I do make it back home – and I shall have to before too long, as the staff and groundsmen must certainly be at sixes and sevens by now – then I'll make sure you get your due credit. There might even be a posthumous medal. An obituary in the *Telegraph*. A gentleman and officer fondly remembered. Yes, yes, I know you haven't admitted it yet, but it's been clear to me from the start. It's why I approached you in the first place. That sense of authority, a certain bearing – quite unmistakable. You think I'd have bothered with you if I thought you were some cloddish tinhat? You might not recognise it now, but it'll come to you in time. We can't change what we are, even if we might like to.

In any case, I wonder if you've even been going about it the right way. Trying to find yourself among those letters simply by poring over them. Better to discover yourself through writing one of your own. Don't you think that makes sense?

The rider pauses for breath. Perfect sense.

Upon which, the notional ex-captain quickens his pace until caught up to his less charitable counterpart, who turns to see the rider following. He cups his hands to his mouth. 'Stronger than you thought, eh?'

The rider takes the deepest breath he dares.

Stronger than you know.

*

The deserters pause, waiting with ill-disguised impatience as the rider slogs towards them. The prodigal pack mule, now no more than an inconvenience. It'll be dark soon, warns Brinkhurst, they really ought to be in the foothills before then. Can't he hurry it up a little?

But he is making his own way now, escaped from their heckling and malice into the quiet hollow of a transport ship, where he finds himself more at ease, despite the stifling air, the stink of diesel. A solitary sort, better schooled in the lexicon of metals than in human nature. A man not unlike Lance Corporal Swann, if truth be told.

And here too there are happier discoveries awaiting: those times when he will look into a crew compartment and find inside it a message from his wife. *Never lose hope, I know you'll be coming home*, or, *everything is waiting for you, just as it was.*

No more treasured moments than these.

'What on God's good earth is that?' Brinkhurst drops the binoculars from his face.

The deserters gather, their attention turned from the colossal reef sliding upward before them to a collection of sheet aluminium and canvas dwellings nestled among its jetties and forelands, the entire settlement ballooned from the sheared fuselage of a transport plane.

'Not too smart,' says Swann, 'whoever they are. Spot those fires a mile high.'

Brinkhurst raises the binoculars again, intent on the softly glowing stretches of hide. 'I don't suppose they care.'

'Refugees?' says Mawdsley, without compassion. 'Chased out of their villages, maybe. Nowhere else to go.'

'Definitely locals,' says Brinkhurst. 'One or two of them outside. God knows why they didn't all hike off into the mountains. Safer up there, you'd think.'

'Scramble 'em out of there,' says Swann, 'and we got ourselves somewhere to shack up. All nice and ready, no bother.'

Brinkhurst's expression sours. 'Well, we don't want a fuss,' he points out. 'No sense making a song and dance of it.'

The matter is deferred for now as they press on towards the mountainside, Brinkhurst taking the opportunity as they draw closer to raise his finger triumphantly towards moonlit inclines decked with foliage, grass, sprays of forest, bursts of white blossom. 'So what do you think about *that*?'

And no wonder at his excitement, thinks the rider, when here at last is his prize of prizes, an unassailable retreat, the end of war. And a kingdom where they are to be installed under his princely rule. A more successful adventure – he might claim – than any battle they might have fought.

They arrive presently at a nook underlaid with veinlike channels of rock and sheltered on both south- and east-facing sides by barricades of red limestone. This will do, announces Brinkhurst. Far enough from the wogs that they won't come begging or thieving. Close enough to keep an eye on them in case they try.

With some eagerness they dump their baggage into the centre of their temporary harbourage, each man at once looking to secure himself a bedroll for the night before they set about lighting a petrol-and-sand burner. A high wind arriving with darkness to whip the flames about, the bitterness of it causing each man's teeth to clatter.

'Fucked if I'm goin' to sit here and freeze,' says Swann, hurling the cold dregs of his tea. 'Not when those monkeys are having a cosy time of it.' He rises and goes to the weapons bundle, unwrapping it to select a Sten.

Brinkhurst looks woefully to the stars. 'Swann, look, I'm not giving you orders, I'm really not. But all we want now is to go unnoticed. Keeping a low profile is what we should be about. Don't you think?'

'I'm bettin' they scare dead easy. Only take a min. What do you reckon? Five at the most.'

They watch him march off, a brooding Brinkhurst pulling his knees to his chin. 'Absolutely farcical. No more wit than the man in the bloody moon.'

Mawdsley stands to gaze after the lance corporal. He asks for the binoculars and raises them to his eyes.

'Let's hear it then,' says Brinkhurst dolefully. 'The usual shoving and stamping, is it?'

The rider pictures it vividly: Swann stalking with Olympian disdain among the downtrodden and sick, eyes fierce with pleasure as he kicks one huddled wretch from his bed, propels another trembling soul out into the cold. Your fucken problem, he'll retort, when tearing a starving family from their blankets. Your bad luck!

Mawdsley continues to watch.

'Just don't fire your bloody gun, you nasty, dunder-headed infant,' mutters Brinkhurst. 'For Christ's sake.'

The archdeacon drops the binoculars. He's coming back! Already, and without stirring anything of the expected furore. A change of heart? The lance corporal famously dissuaded?

'Are there many of them?' Mawdsley thinks to ask when Swann re-enters the camp, his expression unreadable as he makes his way directly to the piled rations to select several tins. He catches Brinkhurst in a quick stare, as if to dare comment, then promptly sets off back in the direction of the shelter.

Brinkhurst shakes his head. Easier to predict the changing wind. A man like that will chew you up if you let him, consume you in his appetite for misrule. Worse still, 'He took the peaches, damn it. No need for that.'

Quietly elated, the rider watches Swann depart. A man thrillingly at war with himself, the very model of confused self-hood. In seeking one's own identity it should come as no surprise to unearth more than a single nature.

He picks up his bedroll and takes himself away from the others to find a more secluded space, his view of emptiness pleasingly obstructed by a low barricade of rock, into which is carved the face of some inscrutable deity, its crudely sculpted features accented in moonlight. The handiwork, perhaps, of some other fellow who had crouched here to shut out the desert. The act of authorship a reliable path to self-discovery, as Brinkhurst had (kindly) proposed.

Except of course one would need a correspondent to be

encouraged to one's best efforts. A wife or sweetheart with whom to share those more personal thoughts and fancies.

My darling——

He might tell her,

I'm alive. Alive and whole, un-maimed, face unscarred, limbs intact. I can walk to you unaided, just as before. Nothing is lost. We can pick up the thread.

I was in an explosion. It damaged my lungs. It's hard to breathe sometimes, but I know you'll understand. It's manageable. The long-term prognosis is good. The important thing is that I'm coming back. We're going to be among the survivors.

And if he might only flesh her out a little, make her more real to him, then he might find more inspiration yet. This more fully realised version of her being a woman of refined taste and enquiring mind, who might appreciate his more philosophic ponderings, his inclination towards the mystic. And beyond that he would presume more of her still: that she is bold, modern, almost wilful in her determinedness. A woman who will dye her hair flame red to signal her unguarded tempers, and who will don her husband's leather greatcoat and ride his motorcycle. And who, by cloaking herself in a fierce obstinacy, will refute those withering claims set out in War Office teletype . . .

REPORTED MISSING PRESUMED KILLED STOP/REPORTED DECEASED STOP

. . . every ounce of her faith cemented instead to that certainty of his eventual return.

My dearest husband,

Nothing matters now. Nothing except that you are coming back to me.

I never believed them when they told me you wouldn't. I never felt you were gone.

So come home and heal, be well and whole again. And we will live our lives. Everything we wanted, everything we planned.

You are my greatest joy, and all I ever wanted.

Yours with all my heart,

xxx

xx

The rider looks up to see Swann, his silhouette ogreish against the moon, his hands stayed in the action of unbuttoning his shorts. The lance corporal cranks his head to one side as if better to study the idol's features. 'Fuck,' he says conversationally. 'Looks just like me.'

He expertly takes aim and pisses long and loud across the face, then ambles away into the dark, a halo of his own expelled air carried with him.

13

The next morning the deserters breakfast perfunctorily, then abandon their nesting place to enter the gape of a broad valley, its rock-strewn base selected as the least taxing route upward. Re-equipped with his load, the rider spies a lizard shimmy across a stone ramp only feet before him. Then mounds of goat scat, a collection of hoofprints, several inlets to rodent burrows. All manner of life returning, creatures barred from the desert's inhospitable reaches harboured here. A haven quite removed from the bordering deadlands.

Further progress takes them onto ground of modest incline, a series of stone tiers incrementing in height, each divided by parched watercourses and seeded here and there with the evidence of human activity; frayed tethers, fragments of earthenware vessels, strips of dyed fabric trodden into the gravel. Between tongues of sandstone that loll out from the hillsides there are miniature hand-built cairns, piled to some practical but unreadable purpose. Burial markers, perhaps, or the wayposts to some preferred passageway into the mountain. The group mount the crest of a plateau to spy a small settlement raised up in warped blocks of clay, each of the several dwellings roofless and derelict. Swann indicates for them to crouch in the cleft of a neighbouring defile until they are certain the site is empty. Then they move on, curious, and in some wonder.

A little farther they find a corpse. The man has been crucified across the breadth of a low-built sangar, each wrist pinned and splintered beneath a basalt boulder. The flesh eaten from his suspended feet, the eyes pecked from his face, the shrunken remainder of him harvested by all manner of lowly creatures. Time and the elements have largely denuded the fellow of his uniform, but it's possible to discern that the cut is Italian.

'Best watch yourself,' quips Swann to Lucchi. 'Not big on macaronis round here.'

The Italian pauses to regard the body, his expression wavering between mystification and horror. An evil man? An oppressor? A murderer of the innocent and the wounded? He hefts the chicken cage further up his back and presses on, followed by the rider, likewise enthralled. It seems almost unconscionable in the moment merely to take note, as though the execution were any mundane feature. But there are mitigations. The man's rank still shows. There are dog tags around his neck, giving his name. He will be found, his story will be made known, along with those famously tortured, who are remembered with greater enthusiasm than the prosaically killed. There is at least that.

They trek on through a wadi, which deepens into a scree-bedded gulley as it winds into the mountains, woodland gradually thickening about its upper reaches. Swallowed up, decides the rider, into some vast mouth of nature where they can lodge themselves, never to be pulled. Their mood ought really to be better. To have the shade of cliff walls cut across their faces, to see the silhouettes of pines! But still there is an apprehensiveness among them, no sense of elation. For himself this might be expected, all natural colour and shade burnt to red, the steppes gathering upon each other as larval flows, sprays of myrtle and juniper blooming into embers. For the rest it must simply be that wariness of the unfamiliar. These formations that tower above them and close off the sky after so much time on open land, rock faces scooped and carved in the fashion of medieval dooms. Even a foreign air now, flavoured with the sweat of vegetation, thickened with pollen. Like any migratory creatures, they must adapt. There's still an hour or so of daylight, reminds Brinkhurst. They should make for higher ground, find a safe vantage point before evening.

They pass into a valley between two forested slopes, its floor thick with rockfall, and under Swann's direction they abandon the ravine's floor to begin their ascent of the hillside. Again the rider struggling to keep up, distrustful of his own body, wary of sudden failure. Even Lucchi clambers past, saddled with his poultry like a doltish bumpkin to market. And then Brinkhurst, with his backpack of vanities. Neither of them pausing to offer assistance or voice concern as he clings vainly to those occasional handholds – an uprooted tree, a node of rock – that prevent him slithering back down into the valley.

He pauses to muster his energy and looks up towards a ledge jutting from the hillside, thinking at first that the figures leaning from it are saplings. When he recognises them as human he freezes. A small group of dark-skinned and turbaned fellows swathed in white cloths, several holding rifles the length of walking sticks. He thinks at first of raising the alarm, then decides against it, urging himself instead to greater haste in recovering the distance to the others.

By the time he pulls himself into their company, he finds the deserters paused upon a narrow escarpment, their observers already noted. 'Senussi rebels,' says Brinkhurst. 'Probably been here since the Ities rounded most of them up for work camps. I doubt they're any threat. Not unless they think we have something of value.'

'That's you fucked then,' says Swann, with unsettling reason.

They move on, casting the occasional, nervous glance upward as they navigate the escarpment to make for the next tier of stone. The Senussi disappearing now and then only to materialise again a little farther across the upper slopes, their path bringing them gradually closer as they keep pace. A rangy half-dozen, thinks the rider, each of them treading with a goat's sureness, their robes overbound with bandoliers, belts tucked with blade sheaths. The classic portrait of banditry, yet lacking that keenness of intent.

The Senussi track them across a narrow vale of sedge and maquis, their route taking them across the wide roof of a hillside cave, its pink-black interior mottled like dog gums. They move with near silence, only occasionally giving reminder of their presence with a quick utterance or the report of a hardwood butt against stone. Weapons-girded Trappists, decides the rider, austere in their devotions. So unremarkable does their shadowing become that by the time the deserters embark upon a narrow causeway, they are careless of the Senussis' presence on the overlooking ridge, their interest presumed by now to be no more than curiosity.

The first stone goes almost unnoticed, taken by all to be a small slippage from the mountainside. And then a second and a third missile clatter down, bringing the deserters quickly to the realisation of an assault, each man cowering and looking to the fellow nearest for example. It takes only a few seconds for it to dawn that there is only one target among them, the hapless Lucchi subjected to a steadily increasing barrage as he struggles to support the chicken cage. One rock strikes him on the shoulder, and another behind the ear. Then one to his shin, the impact causing him to lose his footing and slip to one knee.

Swann swears and puts down the Bren. He unslings the rifle from his shoulder, the action quickly stayed by Brinkhurst. No point in making things worse. We don't have to be involved.

The Senussi hurl more stones, Lucchi raising his hands to

shield his head, the chickens' wild flapping further unbalancing him. Swann continues to watch in silence as the Italian again attempts to stand, another stone glancing off his left knee, causing him to yelp and buckle. When yet another spins off his temple to leave an ugly laceration, the lance corporal is able to abstain no longer. He marches swiftly over to the felled POW and at once positions himself as a shield, daring his assailants to continue with a look guaranteeing all hell should they try.

A further lone missile falls wayward of him. And then stillness, the barrage ceasing so abruptly that the Prophet himself might have appeared to raise a staying hand. The Senussi one by one dropping their arms to their sides before sullenly retiring.

Swann turns to Lucchi, the Italian wiping blood from his eye. 'Come on then. Lazy-arse shite. Up you get.'

The Italian struggles to rise, his knee giving out beneath him as he looks around in bewilderment.

Swann delivers a lazy kick to his hip, unbalancing him further. 'So that's you done for now then, is it? A wee knock and that's your lot?'

He kicks the POW again, the impact causing him to begin sliding from the pathway and down onto the grassed slope beyond.

Brinkhurst clears his throat. 'Swann. We should move on.'

Seeing Lucchi slip further, the rider hurries forward to place a supporting hand beneath his elbow until he can secure his footing. He waits until the POW is back on his feet and withdraws without engaging Swann's glare, leaving the shaken Italian to adjust the cage on his back and hobble to his place in the troop.

Swann watches with scorn, a quick shake of his head signalling the episode closed. He picks up the Bren and leads them briskly from the causeway.

'That might have been a mistake,' says Brinkhurst, close at his heels. 'Those people own these hills.'

'Used to,' says the lance corporal, not looking back.

They climb higher, the circumference of a fading sun sharpening as they move towards it. Surveying the terrain below, they can see a deep threadwork of gorges and canyons, their grooves and bights shrouded by an abundance of forest. There might be fruit trees on the higher escarpments, even orchards. They might see rainfall, the dream of every desert wanderer. Easy now to appreciate Brinkhurst's ambitions towards domicile here, the tricks and confusions of nature so mischievous that no armed force could hope to capture the area fully. The hillsides are overrun with bolt-holes and warrens, hiding places aplenty masked by blinds of camelthorn and tamarisk. They'll be able to blend here as never before, become as unremarkable as any native homesteader or herdsman. Here they might disappear in plain sight.

Lucchi is defeated, able to go no further. The strain and discomfort of the chicken cage, the shock of the barrage upon him. He struggles manfully to pull himself upright after sitting heavily upon a hummock, but after several pained efforts resigns himself, offering only a disconsolate '*Un momento*'.

There's to be no further argument over the chickens, and

Mawdsley is assigned the duty of execution, this time meeting no protest from Lucchi as he lifts the cage from his shoulders. Perhaps, thinks the rider, because the Italian presumes freedom for the birds. Only when the MO drags the first of them out by its neck does he see the intent and raise his voice in pleading, his hands clasped. All that effort for nothing. Mawdsley spins the chicken by its neck, quickly breaking it, and then repeats the same with the second, completing the slaughter as efficiently as tying a ligature. He drops the birds at Lucchi's feet, the POW close to tears. Was there ever so pitiful a captive? The rider regards him with near contempt. A normal reaction, he assures himself, towards the weak and the bullied. A primal instinct rather than any failing of character.

The group move on, Lucchi encouraged by a sharp kick from Swann to take up the dead chickens. They have an objective in sight now, a broad and flat summit standing proud of neighbouring plateaux. Perhaps it will allow them a view of the coast, only a few miles distant. They can make camp there before sundown, then scout tomorrow for a suitable location for their new den. It should all be plain sailing from now on, assures Brinkhurst. Definitely the right thing to come here, no question about it.

But for the rider, their goal might just as well be a mirage, that familiar, devastating depletion of energy once again cutting him down. Though at least this time there is some warning for it, the slowing blood and failing synapses signalled with the onset of blurring vision and light-headedness. He sits heavily then leans onto his side, able this time to raise a short distress call.

Mawdsley moves to attend him. No, he doesn't need water. No, of course he can't get up! What a stupid question. The MO looks to Brinkhurst and gives a small shake of his head.

Brinkhurst sighs and dumps his luggage. They can't go on like this, it's ridiculous. Is this the end of him, or what? The ex-captain points up to the plateau. 'You know where we're headed; you can catch us up when you feel up to it. All clear?'

The rider nods. Quite.

Mawdsley stands over him, crowned with sunlight. 'Don't try to move on until you feel strong enough. Stop if there's any chest pain. And give yourself rest breaks, don't try to make the whole distance at once.'

There's nothing else to be said. Not even the opportunity for the rider to offer any stoicisms, a 'Yes, of course you must go on without me', or, 'Don't worry, I'll be on your tail in no time'. The deserters already returned to their procession towards the mountaintop.

Until Brinkhurst notices that Lucchi is not with them, their POW now seated by the rider, his baggage carelessly thrown off.

The ex-captain drops his head in weariness. 'Swann . . .'

No further complaint is necessary, the lance corporal quick to set down the Bren and advance to the seated Italian, his rifle already unslung. He points the barrel at Lucchi's chest. 'Not fucken going to say it twice. Get up.'

'I stay,' says Lucchi meekly. He points to the rider. 'For him.'

Swann shuffles forward. 'You know I mean it.'

And still the Italian doesn't move, his fingers gripping the rock he sits on. The rider ought to be touched by his loyalty. Rather, he finds it slightly absurd.

Swann lunges out and drags at Lucchi's shirt in an attempt to haul him from his perch. Instead he unbalances himself and tumbles across the Italian in apostolic embrace. Brinkhurst steps forward. 'All right, all right. You can't shoot him, Swann, for God's sake. We can't carry everything ourselves.' He takes the rifle from his shoulder then squats at the rider's side and hands it to him. He nods towards Lucchi. 'If he tries to run, shoot him. Can you do that?'

'Yes,' says the rider. 'I'll shoot him.'

''Course he'll run,' says Swann, dusting himself down. 'They both will.'

'We'll expect to see you at the camp tonight,' continues Brinkhurst. 'We're taking all the food with us, so if you want to eat that's where you'll need to be.' He scrutinises the rider's face for any marker of intent. Then stands and hauls his haversack up about his shoulders before heading off, followed in short course by the archdeacon – who takes up the dead chickens – and a chagrined Swann. Within minutes all three have navigated around a sandstone corbel and vanished into higher forest.

The rider looks across to Lucchi, who offers a thin smile in return. A polite coyness between them where there ought to be a friendship. The rider isn't sure what to say. Thank you for risking death on my behalf, but whatever for? He pulls himself more upright and rests the rifle across his lap. 'You should go now. While you have the chance.'

Lucchi stares at him, making doubly sure he has the meaning.

'That's right. Run. Away from here.' The rider sweeps his arm vaguely outward. 'Bloody disappear. If you have any sense.'

'*E lei?*' asks Lucchi, perplexed. And then: 'I stay.' He holds a brief silence and then begins to gather together the packs and bags at his feet. 'Is better.'

The rider watches, uncertain whether his benefactor is being calculating or asinine. If his plan was to make a break, then his defiance was well judged. But now to remain here, on the grounds of misplaced sentiment? It's addled thinking.

Lucchi gestures towards the rider's postbag. '*Potrei vedere?*' Might I see?

The rider pushes over the bag of letters and watches as the Italian proceeds with an archivist's care.

'*Tutti morti?*'

'Yes,' says the rider. All dead.

Lucchi appears struck by melancholy as he picks up the photograph of Coates. 'Very sorry,' he says, showing the picture. He abandons his search of the postbag and reaches into a pocket of his tunic to withdraw a piece of folded notepaper. '*Potreste?*' he asks. Could you . . .?

The rider nods and accepts the folded paper, glancing at the addressed outer leaf before slipping it into his postbag. Another unwanted commission. The irony of it apparently obscure to all but himself.

'*Grazie. Grazie molto.*'

The Italian proceeds to make a small reconnaissance of the area, the rider wondering whether he means to steal them both away down the mountainside. A prospect which both excites and disturbs him. What if they should encounter the Senussi again, their attack this time pressed to a fatal conclusion? He might be left alone in some casket of leaves to die of cold and starvation. The same fate as Coates. Could anything be worse?

In the event, his speculations are baseless. When he shoulders his rifle and declares himself ready to push on, the POW collects whatever might be carried and leads him in the direction of the deserters' travel. Perhaps more the pragmatist than the rider had thought. He might have explained as much in his letter.

Or perhaps he had simply offered some proof of himself, a spirited testimonial.

Beloved wife,

Know that I am trying to make my way back to you. But it is not easy.

I have been taken prisoner by men who have run from their own army. I will not call them soldiers. They are taking me up to the summit of a mountain, where I think we must sit and gaze at the sea until any sign of war is gone. They say I have done terrible things but you know that it is not in my nature to act against my conscience. All lies will wither.

So I will sit on this peak as they command, and close my eyes to them, and think only of how I might return to you a better man.

. . .

14

The last of daylight is already gone when the rider and Lucchi make their final ascent, the slopes redefined in moonlight. Through a crosshatch of cypress branches the rider can see a sky set with stars, the most prominent oriented as though to map the mountainry they are hung to. Far to the west there must be armies of men huddled in their slit trenches, similarly diverted. To the distant north his wife might be gazing now from her cottage window to the same brilliant vertices. No more than an acute between them, a pittance of degree.

Still they are forced to intervals after each measure of claimed ground, Lucchi waiting patiently while the rider sits to recover his breath. '*Un altro po' di tempo?*' the Italian will ask, when sensing the rider is ready to move on. Yes, we can try again, the rider will say, wondering during his most stubborn efforts if he has ever before climbed to such a height, the thought eliciting a pang of grief for any such triumphs wiped from the record.

Lucchi takes his arm to lead him onto the lower steps of the plateau, tracts of woodland giving way to a thin gravel punctuated by barrows of stone. Proceeding onto level ground, they discover once again a new country, the remnants of some ancient citadel strewn about the summit as its capital. Wind-blunted foundation blocks of ancient halls and chambers, the frames of disembodied archways, crumbled towers, squares described by fractured colonnades. Some elegant metropolis shaken apart and dispersed over the plain as though by divine action. An earthquake, perhaps, or some dreadful tempest. They pause for a time to take in the scope of it, then make their way past laurel bushes into the city grounds, awed by the decayed stoneworks of Gymnasium and Forum, Agora and Prytaneum. They move over mosaicked floors and walkways, peer across the hemispherical cavea of an Odeon and tour a rank of headless and wingless statuary to arrive at the marble prow of a trireme, its shadow laid out in polygons.

Both men take a moment to scan the outlying terrain, neither able to see any sign of the others. But then the city's remains appear to extend over the entire length of the plateau, perhaps several miles in distance. The party could have established themselves at its farthest reaches. The rider catches Lucchi's eye and points a finger northward. They should press on.

They trek over loose earth and through thick esparto grass, careful of their footing, the entire plateau cobbled with debris.

The payload from a single heavy bomber might achieve much the same, thinks the rider. A city eradicated in a single onslaught. Similar scenes might be fresh throughout the countries of Europe, over the length and breadth of Britain. The letter written by Tuck's wife had made no report of raids, but then it had been written months ago. Everything might have changed. The factory she works in might have been bombed, the street she lives on, perhaps even her house. A dreadful notion. How is she coping, this woman whose character he has borrowed from to create his imaginary ideal? How is her health? Is she eating well enough? Is she warm enough? What if those trips outside for water should aggravate her chest ailment?

It's why he has to be away from here. He needs information, reports, testimony. If nothing else, newspapers.

So bedevilling, this absence of proof.

They continue on until their crossing brings them finally to the northernmost ledge of the escarpment. Below it are a series of rock shelves, each dense with broken city, the lowest boundary giving way to a gentle declivity that runs out to the flat coast-lands. Prominent among the ruins is the elongated base of a temple, its plot demarked by pale and severed chimneys, while around it stretches a honeycomb of breached chambers, detached entranceways and cryptic groundworks, tall cypresses here and there ornamenting the collapse. On the highest step there is the raised gyre of an amphitheatre, likely the venue for gladiatorial games. Perhaps if the spirits of its fallen now looked on they would applaud the deserters. Let every combatant throw down his arms! Let all run to sanctuary!

Lucchi points to a steady flicker of light, and they see that the deserters have set up station next to the temple and before a monumental fountain, the flanks of its basin overwatched by a pair of white marble lions. They have a small campfire burning, rolls of bedding unfurled close by. Bold of them, thinks the rider, to signal so readily their presence here.

Lucchi begins his descent, leading the rider via a gullied pathway down onto the steppe and past a stone barrier built up on their right, as if to dam the wave of grassed hillside mustered upon it. Hollowed from the slope's midriff are a series of ragged and irregularly sized tunnels, like the warren holes to some troglodyte palace. Enough to hide an entire regiment of deserters, thinks the rider. Each man burrowed into the rock, wary and aboriginal.

Swann is the first to register their arrival, the lance corporal seated at the campfire with Brinkhurst. He alerts the ex-captain, who looks up to regard the latecomers with a keen eye.

'So where you slackers been?' says Swann as the rider and Lucchi draw near. 'Pickin' flowers?'

The rider looks over their scrappy outpost, supplies dumped haphazardly, food tins scattered alongside Mills bombs, rifles and entrenching tools. He hears a slow, mocking clap from Mawdsley, the archdeacon sprawled on top of the temple's base, his legs dangling, his back against the stump of a column.

'You did well to catch up,' says Brinkhurst. 'Good timing, too, just about to get a brew on.'

The rider notices that the tabletop of a nearby altar is gummed with feathers, a mess tin containing the bones of a chicken carcass laid across the fire's embers. Nothing, of course, set aside for himself or Lucchi. 'Why here?' he asks, passing his rifle back into Brinkhurst's extended hands.

The ex-captain fills a mess tin with water and sets it over the fire. 'Better cover than the plateau. Nobody will travel this far north of the coast road. It's a good spot.'

Lucchi sits himself on a block of stone and begins to remove his packs and bags. Brinkhurst pours two mugs of tea and brings them over, along with some biscuits and jam. 'We'll inventory the food tomorrow,' he explains. 'See what's what.'

'How long are we staying?' the rider asks.

'It's an amazing place, isn't it? Graeco-Roman, I think. Looks like the Ities have been doing some restoration work. We found a small cave with running water.'

The rider cups the mug in his hands, pleased to have the warmth of it against his bruised palms. 'So is this what you were hoping for?'

Brinkhurst looks out across the terrace, his gentler self momentarily evident. 'Actually, yes,' he says. 'This is what I was hoping for.'

With that, he returns to the vicinity of the fire to bed himself down, leaving the rider to ponder the story of their appropriated precinct.

*

The next morning the rider wakes up with a start, certain he has heard the drone of a prop engine. He turns his head to see a honeybee alighting on a sprig of thyme. A bee! He remains quite still as he watches it take pollen from the blossom, the sight moving him almost to tears.

He rises from his bedding to see that he is the last to do so, the others already up and about. Their headquarters put into better order now, the supplies organised into clearly defined depots of food, fuel and munitions. The handiwork of Brinkhurst, no doubt. The rider sees him hanging wet clothing from a guy rope strung between two monoliths, no more respectful of antiquity than any backstreet washerwoman. The instinct and world view of a pragmatist, for all his cleaving to decorum.

Swann is standing on the platform above, stripped naked, busy soaping his freckled and hairless chest, a display of Attic noblesse. And a cleansing none had thought possible before reaching the coast. But now they can enjoy the end of privation, debride at last those cloying layers. Easy to think of it all as a new beginning, if one were so inclined.

The group gather together for breakfast, strips of tinned bacon served up by an uncharacteristically bonhomous Brinkhurst, who is keen to direct their notice to a hazy Mediterranean. To swim in the ocean after such a relentless wilderness: imagine! The rider offers a polite smile, but it is the issue of distance that most captivates. The exact width of the sea crossing to Sicily and then to Italy, the mileage from Switzerland through France and up to the Low Countries, the length of the Channel crossing to

England. The overall and precise span of his journey home. Perhaps he will draw a map when he has the chance, arrive at some estimate of scale. A far happier pursuit than any beach trip.

After breakfast the group disperses, each man free to pursue his own distractions. Lucchi takes an exploratory walk over the settlement, while Swann exercises his impulse to affray by trying, Samson-like, to push over several of the temple columns, his most strenuous efforts in vain. Even Brinkhurst appears to have temporarily put aside any thoughts of security, the ex-captain retreating with his clipboard into the shade of an abutment where he sits to make notes and sketches. A memoir, perhaps, or some Darwinian journal.

The rider collects his postbag and steps past a dozing Mawdsley to begin his own tour of the settlement. In sunlight he finds the terrace stripped of its mystery, the site exposed as a grand folly, its stonework vivid against the panorama of richly grassed hillsides, each topped with thickets of cypress, pine and juniper. He can only guess at the colour of the blossom but decides upon lilac or pale blue, something placid, as befitting a mountain idyll.

He follows a route that takes him away from the encampment and up towards the amphitheatre, where he ascends a stone staircase to overlook the theatre pit. Below are fanned out rows of tiered stone seating, the lower ranks tumbled away into the arena, and he settles on a position among the uppermost galleries to look out over the net of crop fields to the shore.

He pulls his postbag close. What those men would have given for such a sight. To see at last some constraint upon distance, when all had been so confounded here by the immensity of space, the lack of compass. And who could blame them for it? One could hardly come into so strange and spare an empire and presume at once to know it.

But they had come nonetheless, their regiments mustered like the armadas of old. And like many a rash fleet they had come to ruin by their own imprudence, thrown haphazardly upon the guns of the enemy. Tanks exploding with a single burst, crewmen tumbling from their hatches like medieval besiegers blackened by vitriol, vehicles holed, rent and punched backward, left to carbonise as marooned wrecks. Outposts whose stories had paused after antiquity had been taken, held, lost and then retaken at ever higher cost – Benghazi, Sollum, Tobruk – each vying with the other for the greater number of graves. Had anybody even been in charge? What had been his name, this squanderer, this dilettante?

Brought to such a precipice, a man might become awake to superstition. He might tie the laces of the right boot before the left, or stir a mug of tea clockwise only. Certain words might go unspoken, like l—t and f—l, as though artefacts of some forgotten tongue. Yet over all these precautions would rule the principles of physical law. So that a married man might not wear his wedding ring on his finger but instead store it in a tank's rear stowage bin. This because in the event of fire the locker would be subject to less extreme heat, while the detonation of explosive rounds within the crew compartment would result in an inferno of over nine hundred degrees centigrade. The melting point of silver.

He pulls open the postbag, eager again for her letter.

A stone flies past him and bounces its way down into the arena. Startled, he turns to see a shirtless Swann standing on the upper slope.

The lance corporal smirks. 'Had you thinkin' it was the rag-heads, eh, Umpty?' He makes his way down to the stone tiers, pausing to hurl another missile into the pit. He takes a seat next to the rider. 'So, you got any smokes in that bag of yours?'

'I can't smoke.'

Swann nods towards the arena. 'Poor bastards had to do for one another down there. Did you know that? Just so's some rich wankers could lay a few bets.' He leans back and rests his booted feet on the next tier. 'I'd have told 'em to shove it.' He tilts his head back and takes a deep breath. 'Not a bad old spot though, eh? Runnin' water, hand-carved piss pots. Fucken Ritz, near enough.'

'I expect we'll stay a while.'

Swann slaps at an insect on his belly, making the rider start. 'But not you though, right?'

The rider hesitates. What's the intent here? To draw him out? Set a trap? 'I hadn't thought . . .'

'It's no secret. Everybody knows you want out.'

'I didn't think I was allowed. Brinkhurst said . . .'

'Brinkhurst? You think he's goin' to bother lookin' for you? Go off searchin' the whole mountain? No fucken way.' He raises his arms in a stretch. ''Course, he's probably wonderin' what you're goin' to say if you do make it back.'

So, the agenda exposed. 'I wouldn't tell anybody where you were,' says the rider. 'I wouldn't say anything.'

Swann sits up. 'Sure. You'd just keep your mouth shut, right? Maybe deliver those letters you've got there.'

'Perhaps.'

'And you reckon you've got the legs for it? To make that distance?'

'I'm not sure.'

The lance corporal gestures towards the postbag. 'They're all dead?'

'I think so.'

'No more than poker chips to silver-spoon pricks like Brinkhurst. You tell me ...' He points to the amphitheatre's arena. '... How is it any different?'

'People won't see it like that.'

'People? I'd have plenty to say to "people".'

'You could do that. A letter. A statement of some kind. If you wanted to.'

Swann rises. 'Not my style, Umpty. Most writin' I ever did was on fish crates. Neither the use nor the time for it since.'

The rider watches him thread his way from the auditorium. 'Why "Umpty"?'

'Don't know your Morse, eh? Iddy-Umpty. Dot-dash. 'S what y'are, isn't it? A fucken blank.'

The lance corporal descends the steps to the terrace and treks back to the campsite. He takes a swig from his canteen before proceeding to the escarpment's edge, where he gazes out towards the coast. Even at this range displaying that familiar impatience, the undeclared appetite for fury.

Yet he stands as a survivor nonetheless, the rider likewise surviving in his company. In part through chance, but also through that same commitment to self-interest, a willingness to throw others aside. Not a deficiency of will, but the distillation of it. And something he can hardly be blamed for, in fairness. Had he by an alternate quirk of fate been introduced into a braver band, then he might have been differently imprinted upon. Such things effected in the realm of the unconscious, quite beyond choice.

He looks again to the lance corporal, now hawking spit down the mountainside, as though in memory of his former sparring partner. The closest to eulogy, the rider imagines, that he is likely to come.

Later in the morning, Mawdsley is persuaded to assume barbering duties, each man taking his turn to kneel beside the grottoed wellspring while he ministers to them like a Baptist, pouring a tin of carbolic-tinctured water over their freshly shorn heads. Only Swann refuses the MO's attentions, trusting to no one's hands but his own for such a duty. Roused to a competitive spirit, the lance corporal proceeds to bald his

crown in double-quick time then takes his leave, defiantly
monkish.

After lunch the deserters devise a game, Brinkhurst rigging a
tow rope between two opposing columns in the temple to act as
a net. He produces a paper packet of Italian 'Lucky Silk' condoms – *seda profilactica* – from his trove of acquisitions and
proceeds to fill several of them with water from the wellspring.
The ensuing match sees the ex-captain and Mawdsley facing the
rider and Lucky across the net, the objective being to catch and
lob back the water-filled condoms without them bursting; a feat
requiring both dexterity and finesse. Of the four, Lucchi proves
himself the most adept by hurling the balloons back with such
force that they cannot be caught without explosion, causing both
Brinkhurst and Mawdsley to be doused in turn, each soaking
received as a blessing after their waterless voyage. The rider does
his best to join the rallies but even a single volley leaves him
breathless, forcing him after a short time into retirement, his
place taken quickly by Swann, whose earlier dismissal of the
game as 'fucken dumb' gives way to a boisterous display of
one-upmanship as he eggs on team-mate Lucchi. The game at
one point draws to a nervous halt as the lance corporal mis-
handles his throw, causing a swollen condom to rupture above his
head, leaving a skin of rubber hanging from his brow. Then he
breaks into a grin, allowing the others to do likewise. Even the
feted Lucchi permitted to smile. A sanctuary of rare calm, muses
the rider, to instil such amiability.

As the game continues, Mawdsley points out that they are

not alone. A small group of Senussi have gathered along the overlooking ridge, both the elderly and children alike watching with bemusement. Swann breaks from the game to pick up some pebbles to hurl, but is dissuaded by Brinkhurst, who reminds him that 'we're going to have to live with these people'. After the game ends, most of the spectators drift away, leaving only an elderly fellow still squatting, the old man unfazed by Swann's robust warnings for him to leave.

'We should talk to him,' suggests Mawdsley. 'He might know something.'

'Want something, you mean,' says Brinkhurst. 'We shouldn't encourage them.'

'Perhaps he wants to trade.'

'Trade what?'

'Mebbe he's got a goat or somethin',' says Swann. 'Might take a swanky clock for it.'

Brinkhurst sighs. 'All right, I'll deal with it. I'll go and talk to him.' He pauses to address Swann. 'If that's all right with you?'

The lance corporal signals his dispensation with a shrug, and Brinkhurst stiffly trudges his way up the roadway to the higher escarpment. The Senussi stands to meet him, and the two of them soon engage in a conference punctuated by bouts of vigorous and indecipherable gesturing. After several minutes the old man produces from within his robes a piece of paper and hands it over, Brinkhurst examining it briefly before nodding his farewell. He makes his way back down, leaving the old man to resume his watch.

'Haven't a clue what he was blithering on about,' announces the ex-captain on his return. 'He speaks barely any English and only a little Italian. Though he did have this with him.' He hands the piece of paper to Swann, who looks it over then passes it to Mawdsley. 'I did ask him where the person who wrote it is, but he just pointed towards the desert. That's if he even understood me. Of course he won't part with the damn thing, so I'll have to take it back to him. You'd think it was his bloody passport.'

Mawdsley regards the note with dismay. 'This could have been a recce patrol. Or an LRDG unit.'

'Let's not rush into anything,' says Brinkhurst. 'If we decide to move on we need to have a plan. We can use this place for now, take some time to scout the area for any better locations.' And then for Swann's benefit: 'Don't you agree?'

Mawdsley hands the note to the rider, who quickly reads it, astonished that something so casually written could carry such weight:

Nice chap, means well
  Avoid his food though, bloody awful, will give you the runs!
  Cheerio

He hands the note back to Brinkhurst, who regards it as though the very writing of it has been an act of fatidic sabotage. 'He's convinced his English name is "Nice Chap",' says the ex-captain. 'Quite insistent on it.' He shakes his head and then begins his short trek to return the letter, the others watching as he concludes the second meeting with a handshake and then strides smartly back, more out of breath than he would like to show.

'Perhaps he could act as guide,' says Mawdsley. 'If we wanted to look for another place.'

Brinkhurst deliberates. 'He doesn't seem too happy about our POW. If it comes to it, we may have to give him up.'

Give him up. Such a benign expression. The rider looks to Lucchi, still buoyed by the accolades for his sporting prowess.

'Is OK?' asks the Italian.

'Everything is fine,' insists Brinkhurst, the mollification intended for all. 'Look, we're doing everything we said we would. No need to rush into anything. Do that, and we might as well be back out there . . .' He makes a gesture southward.

Both Swann and Mawdsley take a moment to regard the overlooking plateau. Brinkhurst tries again. 'We shouldn't overreact, that's all I'm saying. We've time to consider our options.'

'Scoff's not goin' to last for ever,' says Swann.

Brinkhurst displays a moment of exasperation. 'We'll do what we need to.'

The rationale does little to restore the deserters' good humour, but they are commanded nonetheless by the logic of it, the rider taking little interest as they proceed to discuss improved security for the supplies and armaments, ideas on a defence for their commandeered city mooted without irony. Perhaps because they know it will not ever go to the death, that they can at any time turn and run without further disgrace. In his previous life he might have longed for that same recusal.

In the evening, heavy cloud drifts over the mountains, throwing the site into darkness, obliging all to gather to the rekindled campfire. It's an awkward assembly, such intimacy unprecedented even while in their desert base. But there is little option to do otherwise, any solitary-minded individual running the risk of wandering too close to some hidden drop and tumbling into nothingness. There are no tents to retreat to, no means of privacy, each man's bond with his neighbour suddenly irrefutable.

After they have eaten supper – German sausage meat cooked with strips of American bacon – Brinkhurst breaks out the bottle of Chianti from his collection. By way of a celebration, he announces. Nobody knows quite what to make of the generosity, and Swann watches with some suspicion as the ex-captain pours out measures into each man's mug. But once the wine is served even the lance corporal is lulled by the alcohol's effects, and by the lazy companionability that ensues.

Brinkhurst rises to his feet, mug in hand. 'Gentlemen. I think we should recognise what we've managed to do. And against some odds, I might add. We've got ourselves out of the bloody, stinking desert . . .' he makes an orator's pause '. . . and out of the bloody, stinking war. So here's to a job well done.' He takes a long drink, prompting the others – including a nonplussed Lucchi – to do likewise. 'And I think this is a good time,' he adds, 'for us to remember all those poor sods who didn't get the chance to do what we did. And who are still out there doing their damnedest in a job that was bungled from the very start.' He sits again, a little unsteady. 'No doubt about it,' he concludes more quietly, 'we did absolutely the right thing.'

'How long do you think we might stay here?' asks the rider. A clumsiness, of course, but the Chianti's to blame. Any sane and sober fellow being content, of course, to serve out his sentence of indulgence.

'Can't imagine why you're keen to hurry back,' says Mawdsley. 'They'll only have you up on charges.'

'I was escaping,' says the rider, not quite believing it himself.

'Exactly,' cuts in Brinkhurst. 'Which is what we're all doing. Alexandria is going to be another Dunkirk, you wait and see. All we did was get ahead of the game.' He drains his mug and reaches again for the bottle. 'Jerry will have Russia and Palestine sewn up by the end of the year. By the time the Yanks muck in, it'll all be wrapped up. Anyone can see that.'

Swann holds his cup out for a refill. 'Better off stayin' here. Be a farmer, like the wogs. Or a fisherman. Maybe run a business in Alex.'

'You don't have any family?' the rider asks.

Swann ignores him. Brinkhurst finishes the refills and discards the empty bottle. 'Everybody here has family,' he says. 'Even Mawdsley, believe it or not.'

The MO gets to his feet, excusing himself with the need for the toilet. The rider watches as he leaves the vicinity of the campfire. 'How did he burn his face?'

'Mawdsley, old man!' Brinkhurst calls to the MO. 'Our guest here would like to know how you got your burns!'

'Showin' dirty movies in camp is how,' says Swann. 'Got his-self all excited and set the projector on fire. Burnt the whole tent down. And near enough some other wankers with it.'

Mawdsley makes his way back. A pervert then, as well as an addict. He takes his seat again. 'If you must know,' he says to the rider. 'A flare went off in my face. You could have asked me directly.'

Swann lights a cigarette and extinguishes the match with a masturbatory jerk.

Mawdsley gazes at the rider. 'And what about you? It's about time we settled on a name for you, don't you think? Now that it seems you're on the mend. It must all be coming back to you by now.'

The rider meets his gaze, unsettled. 'Sometimes I think so.'

'Well, then!' says Brinkhurst. 'I said you might recover a little if you came along with us. Didn't I say that?'

Mawdsley leans forward. 'Come on then. Let's have it.'

The rider scans the circle of firelit faces, finding himself the focus of each man's attention. 'I think I might have been an officer. A tank commander. '

Nobody speaks. Swann sniffs and downs the dregs from his mug.

'That is, if it's even possible. To be the same man one was before.'

'It's a conundrum,' says Brinkhurst wanly.

The rest sit in silence, each man waiting for the next to take up the conversation.

Swann yawns and gets to his feet. He lights a cigarette. 'Umpty suits you just fine.' He shuffles from the circle, leaving a bloom of smoke hanging.

15

The air is thicker over the ocean today, an impenetrable haze obscuring the division between land and sea. The rider finds it peaceful to sit on an ancient city wall and look out across the borderless plains, discovering now and then that he is able to forget altogether the idea of war. And easier still with such mundane distractions: birdsong, the bleating of goats, a distant call to prayer. Or the clink of enamelled mugs and mess tins from the vicinity of the deserters' camp. They have their routine now, these fugitive settlers, into which he has relaxed, the practice of indolence refined to an art.

Though it seems that such sedentariness is to be no aid to a clearer mind. He had told the others he had been an officer, but withheld the name. And why? Perhaps because to assume that title would be to invite a version of himself he is not yet braced for. Ironic that he should even be obliged to the attempt when all here are committed to the process of escape, the past no more than an encumbrance to be discarded at will.

But for himself it will not be so easy, each fragment of his story casting its own shadow, every facet reflecting some new and unconsidered aspect of himself. That matured burn to his shin, for example, which had tantalised with a host of possibilities. Any contemplation of it now attended by the spit of machine-gun rounds against steel plate, that vivid capture of sparks and splinters loosed into a turret thick with cordite.

Jesus!

Shit, shit!

Didn't come in!

Everybody all right?

We're OK, we're OK.

Anybody hurt?

The shock of impact always the same: sickening and colossal, the tank heaving on its suspension, a barrage of scalding rivets fired onto those nested inside. And always that portrait of a schoolboy face glossed with sweat and oil, headset askew: is that it? Is this the end of us?

And then that miracle he had discovered when he had looked down at himself, his body unscathed except for a minor graze below his knee. His attention given instead to that delta of glassy skin beside it. The sensation of her fingers as real to him now as when she had first bathed the wound, laid the square of gauze across it, tied the strips of lint. *So a three-inch burn to mark the day. What do you make of that?*

It's not such an ugly scar, he had said of it.

All the same. Luck seems quite the stranger to you.

'Hope you're not expectin' a fucken salute.'

The lance corporal briefly displays a mock-quizzical expression then eases his heavy frame onto the wall beside him. He holds out a folded piece of paper. 'So I wrote somethin'.'

The rider accepts it, perplexed at the submission.

'It's what I want to say. Near enough, anyway. But I'm shit with words, like I said. So I made a list. Just the main points. I reckon you could make a better job of it. Just make it easy to read and I'll copy it out.'

'I can't put myself in your head.'

Swann levers himself off the wall and pulls a cigarette packet from his shorts pocket. 'Just write what I've put. But with better words.'

'Who is it to be addressed to?'

Swann lights a cigarette. 'Doesn't matter.'

'It makes a difference.'

'No, it doesn't.'

The rider makes his resignation apparent. 'When would you want it for?'

'When you thinkin' of leavin'?'

'Soon.'

'Soon then.'

And with this the lance corporal departs, leaving the rider to unfold the note, still taken aback at his unexpected commission.

*

After lunch, Swann nominates himself to mount a one-man reconnaissance of the immediate lowlands, and collects a Thompson machine gun and grenades before plotting for himself a route between the escarpments and down into the valley. Brinkhurst does his best to dissuade him but the futility of it soon becomes apparent, the lance corporal typically disinclined to receive counsel.

Almost as soon as he has embarked on his forage, the sky begins to darken with rain clouds: a cause for elation in the open desert, but now provoking only annoyance. They have equipment set out unprotected: munitions, blankets, foodstuffs. Freshly dried uniforms still flapping in the breeze. The first few drops prompt a hasty effort to gather up the supplies and remove them to shelter, the site of choice being a grotto already in use as a provisions store, its arched entranceway faced by a series of limestone steps, its dimly lit interior large enough only for a few to be seated on a carved horseshoe-shaped bench. The rider does his best to assist, managing to collect and deposit a bedroll and the Bren gun into the cave before being obliged to sit and recover his breath while the others complete the operation. When all are retired to the shelter of the cave they sit and wait a while, no one caring to venture an opinion on how long the shower might last. Mawdsley invites better humour by reminding that at least Swann will likely be caught in the rain and drenched, the idea encouraging a thin smile from Brinkhurst. But when the rain peters out without even soaking the ground, the group are left to disperse in a mood of disgruntlement, Mawdsley and Lucchi abandoning the cave to resume whatever idleness had previously occupied them.

'It'll be the ruin of us eventually,' says Brinkhurst, when the others are beyond earshot. 'This do-as-you-please attitude from Swann. His luck will run out at some point. And then we'll wish we hadn't all whistled to his tune. Especially when there are men here who are better qualified.'

And there's the wound, thinks the rider: the captaincy of a baseborn junior. Naive of Brinkhurst to think he might so easily pull away his own nature with those mere strips of fabric. 'You know I'm planning to leave?' he says.

Brinkhurst leans back, expressionless. 'Have you decided when?'

'In the next few days, probably.'

'I see. And you think Swann will allow it?'

The rider is tempted to smile. That persistent recourse to subterfuge. 'I've no reason to think otherwise.'

Brinkhurst nods. 'Don't take his apathy for a permission. What bores him now will enrage him tomorrow. You can count on it. Anyway, I just hope you're making the right decision. A trek like that without any back-up. No group morale to help pick your boots up.'

As though he had benefited from one so far. 'I want to get back home. Don't you?'

'Isn't home wherever one feels most secure?' Brinkhurst glances to the grotto's entrance. 'Anyway. Better not linger. We'll be accused of conspiring.' He gives a quick smile, as if the idea were ludicrous, then lifts himself from the bench and pulls his shirt straight before making his exit.

The rider rests his back against the cool stone, relieved perhaps that the ex-captain's kinder self had not re-emerged, an obsequious and prying Brinkhurst almost as objectionable as a peevish one. Though it seems unlikely that either might now rescue this shoddy collective from implosion, the endgame clearly commenced. And not a man among them should be surprised at it, each of them running from war while carrying the virus of it in their minds and spleens, the same malignancy persisting even in sanctuary. He looks over the equipment and supplies left on the cave floor, wondering if he will be allowed to provision himself for his journey. Likely not. Better then to avail himself surreptitiously of what he might need. Some foodstuffs, perhaps, a weapon certainly. He glances to the cave mouth then unties the bundle of weapons, sorting through them until he picks out a small leather holster, which he opens to find a German Walther PP pistol, almost genteel in its compactness. He ejects the magazine to check the number of bullets, then tucks the pistol into his shorts and replaces the empty holster. Food will be a greater problem, Brinkhurst's careful inventory taking account of all amounts and quantities. Nevertheless, he feels secure in removing from an already opened tin a small number of oatmeal biscuits which he stows in his pocket, thinking to transfer them later to some private store. It might be possible to return for more if the theft goes unnoticed.

When he leaves the cave, none of the others is within sight, allowing him to discreetly carry away his gains.

By late afternoon the weather has warped again, the last clouds burning away to expose a blistering sun, each man seeking some shade to occupy, all wishing earnestly for the earlier coolness of the day.

When Swann finally makes his return, he appears much the worse for his excursion, hauling himself back onto the escarpment bare-chested, his arms and shoulders showing a web of abrasions. Panting heavily and sodden with sweat, he throws down his equipment at the campsite and then splashes water over his face, uttering profanities at the attritions of his route. It's on everybody's lips of course: if he had only waited until they could have secured a guide, he might have enjoyed a less punishing trek. But then such a patient adventurer would not be Swann.

The group gather to a circle to hear his report while Brinkhurst asks Lucchi to refill all of their canteens. No sign of any other troops, the lance corporal tells them. At least, not in the region of the immediate foothills. Only wild vegetation interspersed with some farmed plots, allotments and orchards. And neither any villages nor townships, just a scattering of clay houses and homesteads, several of them uninhabited. If they wanted they could likely commandeer such a residence without opposition, sink even deeper into cover.

After the debrief they are left to reflect on the implications of Swann's findings. To move into the valley would offer better concealment certainly, but then they would lose their vantage point, the ability to monitor the coastal plains easily. They'll need to consider the idea carefully, counsels Brinkhurst. Factor all possibilities.

The rider listens with disinterest, intrigued only by the idea of escape. Little point in becoming involved in deliberations over a new headquarters when leaving is his only intent. And at the earliest opportunity, before he becomes once more fastened into their intrigues.

He notices that Lucchi has paused in his duty of refilling the canteens and is intent upon the plateau above. The rider follows his gaze to see that the entire overlooking ridge has become lined with figures, a band of white-robed Senussi spread out so as to encompass the vicinity of the camp. Some old, some younger, each man aiming a rifle or handgun at the deserters. All standing in silence, their long shadows tumbling over the escarpment.

He alerts the others, who make no secret of their astonishment. That they should be caught unawares with such ease ... No route of escape open to them, their weapons beyond reach in the grotto.

Brinkhurst sees Swann already eyeing the discarded Thompson. 'Swann, what the hell did you do?'

'Nothin' to do with me! Didn't see a single one of the fuckers.'

Brinkhurst looks again to the watching Senussi. 'All right, well, nobody do anything. Let's just find out what this is all about.' He steps forward and cups his hands. 'Can we help you with something?'

'Maybe it's Lucky they want,' hisses Mawdsley. 'Come back to finish the job.'

Brinkhurst silences him with a wave. Still no reply from the Senussi, prompting him to try again. 'Is Nice Chap with you? May we speak with Nice Chap?'

One of their ambushers stands forward to point with his rifle towards the roadway, where the old man is already making his way down, quite unhurried.

Brinkhurst lets out a long breath. 'Thank God. Soon get this business straightened out now.' He waits until the old Arab reaches the upper tier of the escarpment and advances in greeting, a conversation of sign and gesture quickly striking up between them.

Mawdsley clicks his tongue as he sees the old man point towards Lucchi. 'What did I say? They won't let it go. I knew they wouldn't.'

Swann glances at the anxious Lucchi, who in turn looks to the rider. They'll protect him, won't they? Surely?

Brinkhurst breaks from Nice Chap and heads back to the group while the old man begins to make his way up the road, the matter evidently beyond further diplomacy. When the ex-captain returns, he stands with hands on hips, his head bowed. 'Well, they've no problem with us staying here. None at all.'

'Meaning?' says Swann.

Brinkhurst nods towards Lucchi. 'They want to take him with them.'

'Why?' demands Swann. 'What for?'

'You can guess. The Ities have been butchering these people for a generation.'

'Did you agree?' asks the rider.

Brinkhurst cuts him a hostile stare. 'I wasn't given the impression that it was open to negotiation.'

Mawdsley lifts his shoulders. 'So that's it then. What else can we do?'

Brinkhurst looks towards the waiting Senussi, several becoming restless. He blinks into the sun and clears a run of sweat from his temple. 'Look, it doesn't sit well with me to give a man up like this. But he isn't one of us, after all. Swann, what do you say?'

The lance corporal looks towards Lucchi, then spits. 'Can't do it.'

Brinkhurst glances up to the sky, as though to borrow a saint's patience. 'Swann, for God's sake . . .'

'Bunch of ragheads tellin' us what to do. No way. No dice.'

'For *Lucky*?'

''S not for him,' says the lance corporal, again looking to the machine gun.

'Swann, be reasonable. You can't do anything. They'll cut us down before you even get a shot off.'

The rider looks again to the Senussi, his vision swimming. The air almost too thick to breathe. At least a dozen guns on the ridge. No time even to find cover. He meets Lucchi's gaze once more, the Italian doe-eyed with fear.

Swann takes a step towards the Thompson, prompting a falsetto screech from one of the Senussi, his cry attended by a chatter of hastily drawn rifle bolts from the ridge. Brinkhurst lifts a hand, the tremor in his fingers clear to see.

'Jesus bloody Christ.'

The crack of gunfire causes the deserters to cower, the report of a single shot causing confusion to travel the ranks of the Senussi as each man looks to his fellow for direction. After a moment's stillness, Brinkhurst lifts his hands from his head, his attention going immediately to Lucchi's prone body, a thin smoke rising from the stoved flesh and bone that had been his face. Mawdsley and Swann equally rooted in shock.

For the rider, the moment seems almost unreal. The Walther still smoking in his outstretched hand. His memory of the POW's easy grin overwritten by that single, pitiless instant.

It takes a further interval of quiet for the tension to slacken, the Senussi at last beginning to lower their weapons. The rider dropping the Walther to his side as the deserters look to him with appalled disbelief. When finally there is movement again it comes from Swann, who lunges forward to deliver a blow of such violence that the rider is sent sprawling, the pistol knocked from his grip. The lance corporal picks the dropped Walther up from the grass and ascends the steps to the wellspring, where he fires a further half-dozen shots into Lucchi's body before hurling the pistol up towards the Senussi, the gun clattering uselessly away against the rock.

The rider rolls onto his side, blood streaming from his nose and mouth. His first thought being that he might again be attacked. (Or perhaps attended by Mawdsley?) But no one comes to him, leaving him outstretched on the stone, breathless and spent, a thing of no further value.

16

The rider is made to bury Lucchi. The duty a pressing one, the body likely to fester in such corruptive heat. Brinkhurst picks out a plot on the eastern end of the escarpment where the ground is not too solid, and the rider is left to it, the Italian's body untouched except for the removal of his wristwatch and his boots (Swann fortuitously sharing his shoe size). It's a punishing job for a man of such limited reserves, and it takes him over an hour to excavate to a depth of only several inches. He'll have to stop when it becomes dark and resume again in early morning, those few hours of night giving the opportunity to reflect on his penance. He had expected to be accosted after the murder, perhaps set before some improvised tribunal. But no one had made any accusation, no one even remonstrating with him, summary justice already delivered as a yellow and purple bruise over his left cheek and a blackened eye. He had saved all of their lives, and they knew it. A single sacrifice for the greater good, the pragmatism of it beyond question.

For the umpteenth time he loses his grip on the spade and slumps alongside Lucchi's body, obliged once more to consider what manner of man might commit such an act. A coward, some might claim, acting only in craven self-interest. But then had he not also spared their POW? From the terrors of a mob, from awful suffocation at the end of a noose? Had he been able to pick for himself, the Italian would surely have chosen the same. Been grateful for it, even. In the end he had at least taken a path, when indecision might have been the greater crime.

When he has dug a little deeper he receives a surprise visit from Mawdsley, who comes to sit on a nearby section of wall. The archdeacon content for a while to observe as the rider scoops spadefuls of stones and clay.

'So you're leaving, I gather.'

The rider pauses to lay his weight upon the spade. 'You're going to tell me I won't make it?'

'I think you've proved rather a difficult sort to predict.'

The rider returns to his labour.

'Though one might reasonably expect,' continues the archdeacon, 'that a fellow would want to make the best explanation he can for himself. After such an odd adventure, after all. I mean, why not? Why not come out of all this and be the hero?'

'I don't want any attention.'

'Of course not. But all the same, the opportunity . . .'

'To do what?'

'To clean up one's story, so to speak. Perhaps even to report any who weren't so upstanding or dutiful into the bargain.'

The rider spares him a quick glare. 'I'm not going to report you. I never met you.'

Mawdsley gives a sardonic smile. 'True in a way, I suppose.' He leans his head back and closes his eyes. 'This is the only tolerable time of day in this place, don't you find? When everything is losing its heat. About the only time one can ever think clearly.'

'There's something else you wanted to say?'

'As a matter of fact, yes.' The MO points to the unfinished grave. 'I should think you'll want another few feet in depth there. Don't want the poor sod sprouting after you've gone, do we.'

The next day Nice Chap makes a return visit to the camp, bringing news. It happens while the rider is concluding his burial duties for Lucchi, and he is left to speculate on the excitement from a distance as the deserters huddle in conference. Finally it is Brinkhurst who comes to him with an announcement, the ex-captain allowing a short silence as he watches the rider shovel dirt into the pit, each measure further obscuring the Italian's body.

'I'm telling you this as a necessity rather than a courtesy,' he begins, 'since you've shown yourself no more deserving of consideration than any common blackguard. Some of Nice Chap's cronies have reported new arrivals down near the coast. A bunch of Ities in a truck. Half a dozen, at least. Seems like they might be making a camp down there. Nice Chap thinks they're on the trot.' He pauses as if to give the irony its due weight. 'Based on what we've been told, that could very well be the case. No sense in such a small unit being sent here. So they've either become separated and got lost, or he's right. Either way, they're a risk.'

He stops again as the rider finishes his task and steps back from the grave, allowing the opportunity to offer a token valediction. If only because the Italian had travelled the road with them for so long. But he eschews the moment, resuming his briefing with a short cough. 'Of course, Swann is all for making a recce. And on this occasion, I'm inclined to agree. We need to know what this lot are about. How many, what their intentions are. It's a fair old trek, but Nice Chap says he can guide us.

'Anyway. We may need whatever strength in number we can muster. So you'll be coming with us. Probably be hard going for you, but there it is. You'll just have to give it your best.'

He briefly accords Lucchi's grave a pall-bearer's respect then carries himself away, hands folded at his back. Leaving the rider stirred by the prospect of open country, of a territory beyond the fiefdom of his captors. He'll have few better opportunities than this to press his ambitions. An outcast fixing his course to the coastal graph, tracing the lip of land until reaching some port of embarkation. The possibilities are tantalising.

The expedition is scheduled to begin in under an hour, light rations distributed alongside a weapons pack for each man. Fortunately the heat is less intense today, making the burden of kit-bags and weapons less taxing. The rider is given several magazine pouches and a bag of charges but no fireable weapon, barred as he is on grounds of irresponsibility and fickleness from any means of defence. The Senussi look on with a patient detachment, Nice Chap having gathered about him a retinue of three bodyguards for the journey, each taking turns at a long smoking pipe passed ceremonially between them. Each man without discernible expression, notes the rider, as though their faces had been abraded through hardship to a blank physiognomy, leaving one to infer a character from what spare features remain. It might fall to one of these stoic fellows to provide assistance, should he fall behind. Or perhaps – more likely – simply to leave him, the penalties for compassion no doubt already learnt.

When the party sets off, Nice Chap takes his place at the head, attended at close quarters by a steel-helmeted Swann, while the rider brings up the rear. They form a narrow troop as they trek upward to cross the plateau at a diagonal, then file down a gently sloped incline onto a single-lane metalled road. Swann looks up with some annoyance as they pass beneath the shade of overhanging pines, ruing no doubt the punishments of his own route when he might have chosen this less taxing one.

The road delivers them at length onto a broad and open hillside tufted with vetch and thin-bladed grass, any profusion of forest wiped from below this high watermark. For the deserters there is some chariness at being so exposed, while the Senussi press on without pause, seemingly unconcerned to be hares in a hawk's eye as they lead the patrol down towards more level ground. There is a stiffer breeze now, rushes of ocean current

washing against the higher inclines, and the rider finds it invig-
orating, a reminder that they have passed beyond the margins of
the desert into a realm of more animate airs.

They move onto a long secant of red earth, overturned here
and there to make small allotments for the growing of vegetables.
And from here they can see some scattered evidence of civilisation; a few clay blocks for houses, some fenced pastureland, a
corral for two tethered goats. They are joined from nowhere by
two young Senussi boys, who follow with curiosity until, embold-
ened, they run to the front of the group and push noisily ahead,
waving gaily coloured scarves as if to herald some carnival.
Brinkhurst, unenthused at the company, moves forward to
express his concern to Nice Chap, who listens carefully and then
does precisely nothing, leaving the chastened ex-captain to settle
back in line, his ineffectuality recorded with a doleful stare from
Swann.

As they proceed onto a grid of parched arable land the youngsters drop away, instructed at last by Nice Chap that their
adventure is over. The rider is already toiling behind and struggling to keep the pace, his lassitude more than matched by that
of Nice Chap, who suddenly announces the need for rest. He
waits beneath the shelter of a camelthorn tree while one of his
lieutenants unfurls a reed mat for him, then seats himself to chew
absently on a piece of bread, gazing into some imagined abyss
while the deserters look on, long-faced and irritable. Brinkhurst
tries to elicit from him an estimate of how many more miles they
must travel but the old man seems vague on it, moving his palms

apart and then together again, as though the precise figure might be in flux.

After a twenty-minute break the group pushes on, Nice Chap restored to something of his former vigour. Over a stonier and more undulate base now, slabs of bedrock rearing as if to draw back from an encroaching ocean. Veering westward, they tack to the course of a wadi, the base of its channel thick with tall shrub and sedge, and cover another mile or so towards the coast before halting again beneath a clutch of sheltering cork oaks. Nice Chap summons Brinkhurst forward for an impromptu briefing and scores out a small map in the sand, indicating the Italians' position.

'Not much further now,' relays the ex-captain, after several fruitless minutes at his binoculars. 'Sounds like they've driven their transport into the mouth of a wadi and camped a little way beyond it. Too much cover to see anything yet, but we should make contact shortly. So try and keep any noise down. They might have lookouts.'

The rider watches as the three deserters ready their weapons, Brinkhurst breaking his Enfield's breech to do a dry-fire while Swann ensures a smooth feed on the Thompson's box magazine before refitting it and pulling back the bolt. Mawdsley dispenses Mills bombs from a haversack to both, the MO catching the rider's eye as he chambers a round in his rifle, his fingers in fine oscillation.

'Let's try not to stir anything up that we can't deal with,' reminds Brinkhurst. 'This is just about sizing things up for now.' He looks pointedly to Swann, who glowers but holds his tongue.

They move on, the deserters taking up positions abreast of the column and tracking the banks of the wadi until it begins to deepen and widen, allowing them to find better cover nearer its foliaged bed. A little farther on, Nice Chap signals that his journey is concluded, and, along with his bodyguards, turns back. The rider watches him go, impressed by the Senussis' wiliness in dealing with the Italian threat. Set one faction against another and discreetly withdraw: what could be more efficient? Though if the same thought had occurred to the others they must have either dismissed it or simply accepted it, obliged as they are to defend the pack territory.

The rest of the party press forward with greater wariness, weapons held ready as they attempt to find quiet footfall amid bracken and gravel. Tall junipers provide shade and cover but do no work to fend off the heat, each man curtained in sweat as they file along the groove of rock, their forearms and legs raked by thickets of tamarisk. They wind through several further bends in the wadi, pausing before venturing onto each new and unscouted stage, Brinkhurst quietly reminding all to keep scanning the high banks for any sign of sentries.

After a further distance they come upon a heavier dispersal of brush, and Brinkhurst signals caution as they spy a cleared area beyond, unoccupied for the moment but with an extinguished cooking fire at its centre, some mess tins and mugs laid nearby, several bedrolls laid out. At the camp's far side a Fiat truck is parked, its tarpaulin-covered cargo bed and cab overlaid with scrim net and sprigs of bush. Swann directs Brinkhurst's attention to a rifle and light machine gun rested up against the truck. An opportunity, then, the advantage of surprise open to them. Swann points again, this time to a small stockpile of ration tins and boxes set out in the shade of the wadi's banks. The reward for their enterprise suddenly more enticing. 'We can use that truck for cover,' he whispers, prompting a grimace from the anxious Brinkhurst.

But too late for any argument, the lance corporal already moving through the branches, pushing them aside with one hand while gripping the Thompson with the other. The rider and Mawdsley both look to Brinkhurst only to see a helpless shake of his head. The inevitable consequence of indiscipline . . .

On the verge of making his trespass into the camp, a small stone catches Swann on the thigh. Surprised, he turns quickly enough to glimpse one of the Senussi boys who had earlier followed, his face bobbing from behind a bush on the wadi's sloped face. Another missile lands near the lance corporal's boot, its trajectory betraying an accomplice. He jerks his thumb in fury towards the bank. 'Fucken get rid of 'em!'

Spurred to action, Brinkhurst rushes to the slope, shooing and waving his arms as though to flush grouse, his efforts serving only to make the two youngsters bolt from their hiding places and make for the camp. He seizes the smallest as he tries to scrape past, clamping a hand over his mouth while the boy's confederate bursts through the foliage and onto open ground. Swann curses and moves quickly after him, undeterred by the urgency of the ex-captain's warning. 'Swann! Let it go.'

But then the boy inside the camp halts abruptly, his attention shifted suddenly towards his own feet. Swann likewise pulling to a sharp stop as he spies the two clusters of fuse prongs above the surface of the sand, the boy's foot stretching the barely visible trip-wire between them.

'Swann! It's no good. Just leave it!'

The lance corporal stands unmoving, his gaze alternating between the Senussi boy's frightened eyes and his ensnared foot, the wire lodged between his toes and the sole of his sandal. A single tug likely to cause both mines to bounce to waist height to hurl their barrage of shot.

'Swann!' hisses Brinkhurst, the boy squirming in his grasp. 'Come *on*!'

They hear voices beyond the truck, the sound of high-spirited chatter growing louder, causing the trapped boy to look up in alarm. Swann raises his hands in assurance. 'All right now, just keep it steady. Right where y'are.' He edges closer until near enough to bend and examine the terrified youngster's foot, gently feeling the tension of the wire. No give at all. He rests back on his haunches, a triangle of sweat darkening the back of his shirt. 'S-mines,' he calls to the others, as loudly as he dares. 'Mawdsley, you still near that acacia? Need a couple of thorns here, bloody quick.' He looks up at the boy. 'You just keep dead still. 'S all you got to fucken do. OK?'

Mawdsley squeezes through the brush and hurries over, dropping several of the small spines into the lance corporal's open palm. A sudden noise from the other side of the truck alerts both, and the MO drops to a kneeling position, his rifle raised.

'Swann, we don't have time!' insists Brinkhurst, still behind cover.

The lance corporal pulls off his helmet and slides onto his belly, bringing his face near to the leftmost of the mines. He scoops away a little gravel from around the plunger shaft, exposing a small pinhole, then takes one of the acacia thorns and gently slides it into the hole. He allows himself a deep breath and signals Mawdsley a quick thumbs-up, then rolls over to the second mine to begin the same operation.

The Italian soldier who arrives on the scene freezes in surprise, the ghost of a smile lingering even as a bullet from Mawdsley's rifle splinters his breastbone, punching him backward against the truck's cab.

Swann flinches, a thorn escaping his grip to tumble into the sand.

A second Italian appears, pistol already drawn. He skids to a halt by the truck's grille and immediately looses off a shot at the boy, who tears himself free of the trap. The sound of gunfire obscuring Swann's gasp of dismay as the mines jump up from their rooting. A drumbeat of air pressure, the staccato report of steel, fabric and glass as the truck is peppered. The pistol-wielding Italian collapses with a shriek, his hands pressed to his face.

Swann blinks and looks down at himself to see dark spots appearing through his sleeve. Through the dust he picks out the boy already pawing his way through the screen of brush, trailing a stiff and bloodied leg. And then Mawdsley, the archdeacon rolled from his kneeling position onto his side, his bared back mottled with lesions, as though the handiwork of an overzealous blood-letter. The MO groans and calls Swann's name but the lance corporal is already grappling for the Thompson, bringing the machine gun about as more of the Italians arrive. He sends a burst of fire across the bows of the truck, forcing them into cover, while Brinkhurst joins the defence, taking aim between the branches.

'Swann! We're pulling back!'

'Don't you fucken dare,' roars the lance corporal. He stumbles over to Mawdsley and tries to drag him, the attempt eliciting a mournful wail. Rounds spring up dirt by his ankle and he again sprays the truck with fire. 'Brinkhurst! You hear me? Don't you fucken run!'

But too late, the ex-captain already making haste along the base of the wadi. The Senussi youths fleeing ahead, the wounded boy limping as best he can. The rider ducks as he hears shots whistling by, the crack of severed branches. An equine squeal as a bullet finds sheer stone. Swann crashes through the veil of bushes alone, red-faced and sweating, and drops to one knee to unclip a grenade from his waist belt. He tosses it to the rider and barks, 'When I say!'

Raising himself to a stooping run, the lance corporal weaves his way from the camp, the rider at his heels. He pauses to pull the pin from a second grenade and lobs it in a wide arc across the intervening ground, crouching as the explosion lifts a shroud of dust and leaves. They hear one of the Italians moaning. Or might it be Mawdsley? Swann yells for the rider to do likewise, watching as he pulls the pin from the grenade. And then a flicker of hesitation, the rider's arm momentarily in stasis. It's a question of inclination, a longer throw placing the detonation nearer the truck, sparing the MO. A shorter one resulting in the opposite.

Perhaps the archdeacon is already dead.

Swann shouts again and the rider makes his throw, a weak pitch that lofts the grenade only just over the dividing brush, the resulting explosion sweeping up a wave of grit. No sound emerging through the smoke this time.

Swann cuts him a baleful glance and then lifts himself up into a run, his boots spooning sand as he tracks Brinkhurst's retreat. The rider rises to follow but is halted at once by a tide of dizziness, the severity of it leaving him to sway as though bedded in a shifting floor. Desperate with fear, he throws himself into a stagger, reaching for balance with each step. *Where are they?*

Then there is Swann! On his knee again, the Thompson spitting out casings. And there, Brinkhurst, sunk behind a sandstone bulkhead, pulling frantically at his foot, as though it ought somehow to detach. And in the distance, two slender boys in tandem, canted like the dark solidi of a cave mural.

'Give me a hand!' Brinkhurst, tugging still at his ankle, his booted foot disappeared into a thin chasm of rock. 'For God's sake!'

The Italians are moving up the wadi now, throwing themselves from wall to wall, loosing off a barrage of fire. Brinkhurst yelps as a scatter of bullets punches debris from the wall above his head. With a hoarse cry he pulls his foot free and returns fire as the rider wanders past him, clinging to crags and abutments as he tries to follow the retreating Swann. There isn't going to be time. There just isn't.

He rounds a turn in the wadi to see a sliding trail of rock and gravel, and looks up at the lance corporal heaving himself to the top of the banking. Too steep for him to follow, surely. He totters over to the same spot and attempts to mimic the escape, his legs wading uselessly against dislodged earth. He gains then slips, slips then stumbles, grasping for some handhold. Swann looks down at him, panting, his face screwed with fatigue.

'Umpty,' he says.

The rider clasps the Scot's outstretched arm, finding at last some purchase beneath his feet. He claws and scrabbles against the face, sand scuffed into his eyes, a last surge lifting him finally to the summit, where he rolls onto his back, his chest burning, his breathing short. From down in the wadi he hears Brinkhurst's voice, shrill with pleading. He's hurt his ankle, he can't scale the bank! Quickly, for Christ's sake!

Swann helps lift the rider to his feet and they hobble away from the edge as more noise erupts in the trench below, the rattle of machine-gun fire joining the echoes of pistol shots. They hear a short silence followed by a tumult of voices as the rider gazes in disbelief back to the wadi, still half expecting to see the ex-captain or Mawdsley scrambling clear. Could it possibly be true? Their company so quickly and bloodily halved? All duplicity and double-dealing at last purged?

Swann continues to lend his shoulder, drawing them both away from the commotion and back towards unbroken ground. There is no telling how much distance they cover and how quickly, but the Jebel foothills grow nearer every time the rider lifts his eyes. Soon there'll be forest again, and hedgerow, and a thousand places in which to rest, to recuperate and to hide. The scent of blood just strong enough to keep him from unconsciousness.

A single shot causes both men to pull up and look to their rear, the sound no more than a matchstick crack at this range. But there's nothing to be seen, the landscape as inert as the sky, leaving the rider to wonder if they might just have received the final chapter of their ex-captain. A bullet to the head perhaps, from captors immune to his sly diplomacy, his desperate attempts at barter. He would have offered them anything, promised anything, passed to them the deserters' identities, ranks and location like the trinkets he had so jealously coveted.

'Best push on,' advises Swann.

The rider feels weak, nauseous, unwilling even to contemplate the rigours of the remaining journey. 'They might know about the camp,' he says weakly.

The lance corporal winces as he flexes his arm. 'Count on it.'

They muster themselves for the remainder of their retreat, both looking for a final time in the direction of the ground they have fled before moving off.

It is early evening by the time the two survivors make their return to the metropolis, their ascent lengthened by frequent rest stops for the rider. Both arriving back with the expectation that their base might have been ransacked as part of some Senussi plot. But in the event they find everything exactly as they had left it, leaving both to sit in dolorous mood as Swann bathes and dresses his wounds.

'So what happened to you back there?' the lance corporal asks. 'In the wadi.'

'I lost my balance.'

'It goin' to happen again?'

The rider hesitates. 'I was thinking I would leave,' he says. 'And not be a burden to you any more.'

'Goin' to wait until mornin'?'

'First light, I'd thought.'

'Done that letter for me yet?'

'I can do it now, if you like.'

'Fine.' Swann flexes his bandaged arm and gets to his feet. 'Leave you to it, then.'

A little relieved, the rider fetches his postbag and writing implements and sits to his task beneath a setting sun, struck by the irony that this will be the only meaningful exchange between them, both having engaged with one another as a mere necessity. He had given no thanks for his rescue, and likewise had received no censure for his cynical throw. But then the lance corporal would perhaps be the last to expect reason or excuse, his own decisions to save the Senussi boy and condemn Brinkhurst drawn from that same universe of insoluble equation and indeterminate precipice, everything submitted to the cusp of the moment. No wonder then that he cannot find his place.

Swann's table of contents unfolded before him, the rider sets himself to the letter.

The following morning the rider wakes at dawn to find Swann already up, and the two quietly breakfast while the lance corporal takes a little while to read the completed letter. Despite the occasional frown of puzzlement and several sideways glances at its author, he gives it his unspoken sanction and proceeds to the chore of writing it out in his own hand, ink soon spattered onto his hands and shirt as he battles with a recalcitrant pen. The rider meanwhile is given dispensation to pick from the grotto a modest quantity of provisions and a gun, his choice being a weighty but reliable Mauser pistol. While making his selections he comes across the bag containing the ex-captain's treasures and quickly sifts through it, finding nothing of practical use. Hard to think that Swann will find any of the trophies of interest either, the entire collection no doubt destined to gather as refuse among the city's walls and columns.

His preparations completed, the rider revisits Swann to find that the official version of the letter is ready for him to accept into his postbag along with the pen and ink bottle, the lance corporal disavowing any further need for either. He casts a final look about their empty headquarters. 'So you think you'll stay here?'

Swann shrugs. He pulls a cigarette and lights it.

The rider offers a final 'Good luck', the sentiment only half meant. He pulls his postbag up across his shoulder and turns his back on the city, leaving the lance corporal to his smoke.

He makes his way up from the lower escarpment and then over the brow of the adjoining hill, following the prescribed route of descent. For the next several hours he treks across the broad sweep of foothills, ensuring that he swings well to the east of the Italians' domain, pausing occasionally to steady his heart in the bursal faults of granite and limestone plates. In the early afternoon he broaches the last drop of land before the ocean, a craggy bulwark that runs along the sea's perimeter, divided sporadically by water-less estuaries. He pauses on the flat clifftop, shading his eyes to look along the length of an empty coastal track. Then begins his steady climb down, elated to recognise himself as a vessel without fixed course, free at last to contrive his ideal bearing.

17

What liberty! What licence! He's away and out of it now, unbuttoned from any interest but his own, loosed like gunsmoke into the wind. Enough provisions to stand him for several days, a sketch of the country copied out: Benghazi to the west, rumpward of the peninsula, Derna located eastward, the ribbon of seaboard winding out to Tobruk, Mersa Matruh and at length the port of Alexandria. The entire journey perhaps some five hundred miles, a farness of dispiriting reach given his few supplies and limited endurance. But if he approaches it with the idea of a campaign, gathering the distance in stages, then fortune might carry him on.

He walks for a time along the frontier of cliff running parallel to the shore, a rough cart track the only feature between himself and the ocean. At first he stays close to the shelter of higher ground, wary of any aerial reconnaissance, but before long he finds himself unable to resist the sea, and crosses the track to survey the pattern of coves and inlets that break occasionally into stretches of unspoilt sand. In need of rest, he finds for himself a comfortable vantage point overlooking a small bay, and he removes his weapons and kitbag to sit for a while, beguiled momentarily by the intrusions of a former life. The quiet harbour of some seaside getaway or postcard resort, the specifics of location and circumstance obscure to him, the indices of time and place not yet repaired. It occurs to him that the act of swimming might help rebuild the missing connections. But his ears are perforated, his muscles lacking the strength to push through any undertow. So he must accept for now his limitations, and be content to imagine.

A flight of aircraft passes overhead, their low-frequency drone causing him to stir. Enemy planes, to judge by their eastward path. But too far above to see him, their target in any case certain to be more pressing than any lone foot soldier. Most likely they are bound for allied shipping convoys, or the dockworks of Tobruk. Perhaps the shipping lanes of Alexandria, or the training camps and supply depots outside Cairo and Giza. How many tons of TNT to be dropped? How many millions of mines to be laid? Enough to refigure the landscape of a country, its map studied now as a means to strategy, its place names overlaid with the icons for airfields and fuel dumps. And perhaps the same now for any implicated nation, shocked and battered into transformation. Who could possibly expect to emerge from such a cataclysm unchanged? No need for him to feel estranged or set apart from the common experience. He must find his way home exactly as the rest, bewildered and unsure, encouraged by hopes of a more certain world.

He lingers to watch the surf rise against the rocks, diverted briefly by the fantasy that enough bombs might fall to sever the entire cap of land, setting it to sea like a colossal raft, bearing him homeward. Then with a gust of effort he breaks from the idea to take up his luggage, and commits himself once more to travel.

Further eastward the range of tall bluffs slides away into flat arable land, many of the plains apportioned into small and irregularly sized cornfields, putting him in mind of human skin through a magnifying glass. North of the coastal track a gathering of clay and thatch dwellings begins to multiply, and he decides it safer to move away from any centres of civilisation, the loyalties of their inhabitants unknown. In the afternoon he treks a little further inland to pick out a rest spot in the shade of a line of blossoming cacti. The profusion of flowers – which he thinks might be yellow – so great that each mast might have been garlanded to mark out some festival ground. Many of the paddles are crested with a number of small and rough-skinned fruit, and he picks several to put into his kitbag, thinking to sample them in the event of keener hunger. The rows of cacti have been set as hedgerows to divide the lands of neighbouring farmers, and he looks on as several of the harvesters take again to their labour, an aged fellow scything corn with a hand sickle, a black-shawled

woman carrying a basket between olive trees. Portraits of rusticity to rival any medieval woodcut. Occasionally he receives a
curious stare from those who pass by, but no one pauses to offer
any greeting, a conflict between foreign powers likely no more
comprehensible to them than a war in Heaven. If they might
upheave themselves and make a push towards civilisation they
would find their roads holed, their bridges blown and their wells
salted. But most will not venture so far, sealed as they are into an
existence indentured to inches of rainfall, a summer's yield of
grain. There might be a peace in such a life if one were an uncom-
plicated man. A man like Swann, for example, who knows
himself so well that he might comfortably abstain from the wider
world. But one would need to be certain in such a demission,
untroubled by any ties to family or loved ones. And in composing the lance corporal's letter the rider had only discovered further
proof of himself, the casualness of the farewell entirely contrary
to his own nature, his every retracing of the words leading him
to marvel that he could ever have stitched himself into that same
impenetrable skin:

Dear——,

– the intended recipient having never been divulged to him –

*I wanted to write and let you know not to worry when you do
not find me returned home with the regiment. It is not because
any harm has come to me but because I have decided to stay*

here. I think it is the best thing for me. This is a wide country, and once the war has blown past there will be plenty of space for a fellow of big ideas to set out his station and make a go of it. I will miss you and Hettie and granda but I will not miss the boats or the docks or the pier or the thin streets. I will not miss the low sky or the sight of fish heads mashed into the cobbles. It will not trouble me to think that I have run my last errand to MacQuarie's stall, or that I will never again knock a man into the freezing sea at Christmas. And apart from one or two who might notice that extra quiet in my dens of habit, I do not think that I will be much missed. So let there be no upset.

I should warn however that you may come to hear reports of me that are not true and that I should not want you to believe. This is because I have resigned from the army and have yet to let them in on it. But you know how it goes with me. I have no more care for a captain's bark than a headmaster's clout, and I will not work against the grain of my own nature no matter what the penalty. The army is managed by a clan of ditherers with swagger canes and perfumed cheeks, and I cannot find it within myself to run and fetch and carry and die for the likes of such. We have been thrown forward and backward like a tug in high seas according to the whim and guess of these sorts, and have gathered no advantage other than to collect the odd patch as minefield or cemetery. It is the worst kind of waste, and too sad to see, and so that is why I have made myself my own man.

If the papers should come to you for any statement (or if you *should feel compelled to put yourself forward in my name), I should be obliged if you might bring to their attention the following with respect to our troubles here:*

i) That our boys need better equipment, including guns of greater calibre and range, so that they might at least hold their own in open contest.

ii) That we need more and better armoured vehicles, our woeful collection tossed at present into the ring to be squashed like old hats and then set to burn, with terrible consequence.

iii) That training camps should be built to a higher standard of cleanliness and safety, with less risk of infiltration by insects, snakes and especially scorpions (which are the very worst and most malicious of all creatures that scuttle or crawl).

iv) That whoever is running the whole show should be hooked from the stage as would be any inept vaudevillian and replaced with a man of foresight and frugality. A Highlander would be a commendable choice.

Other than the above, it remains only for me to wish you the most profitable and happiest of lives, and to ask of you a final favour, which is to at some point (and at your convenience) seek out Conall MacKeown, who is the eldest of the MacKeowns on Balfour Street, and to batter him enthusiastically about the face. I have thought many a time to administer this correction myself, but the job has somehow escaped me. Be assured that such a thing would be a charity not only to me but to all who have ever met him, or are yet to do so.

Finally, please do not think that I am suffering any

hardship here, because I am not. Instead look to your
lanterns next time they blow out in a storm and think of me
watching fireflies against a desert sky. All will be well, and
for the best.

> *Your dearest——,*
> *Rolland*

Not authentically Swann, of course. Certainly no version of
him that friends or family would immediately recognise. But
the lance corporal had nevertheless seemed satisfied with the
reinvention of himself into a more erudite and expressive lout.
Perhaps in the end he had simply wanted to send something
back to demonstrate that he had somehow become a better and
wiser man than he had been before, found amid war some well
of learning and knowledge from which to invigorate and better
himself. Lance Corporal Rollo Swann will indeed be going
home, but as a revised version of himself, a man of letters and
of scholarly perception, this palimpsest now destined to enter
the collective memory. Philanthropist and humanitarian, a bluff
and hearty rascal with wit to spare. While somewhere at the top
of a nameless summit the real Swann might gaze out, brooding
and Hyperborean, restless as an exiled king. The truth of a man
lying somewhere between who he was and who he might yet
become.

Exhilarated by this reasoning, the rider resolves to take up his
journey once more, his path plotted out after the aspect of a

natural fault, making the straightest cut possible across the broad head of land.

He walks through the afternoon and into early evening, tracking as far as he dares from the coast while keeping it in sight. Southward of his path a series of low hills rises up, their slopes and valleys dense with juniper and fine-bladed sedge, each billow of land rendered in bright copper under a fading sun. By dusk he reaches that part of the coast which falls southward again, where he tracks the ellipse of a crescent bay. Moving further up the hillside he encounters the ruins of an ancient basilica, and he approaches the site with some caution before reconnoitring the grounds, pausing only in admiration of several cracked floor mosaics. Afterwards he collects kindling for a small fire and heats a tin of M & V skilly and some water for a mug of tea, and reclines to ponder a flotilla of stars. The very spot, he imagines, where men of faith must have stood and ruminated. God now and then spied amid an unworked nature.

In the morning he struggles to free himself of a stiffness which has set intractably into his limbs. The result of pushing them while deprived of fuel. He will need to slow down, measure his pace to the limits of his body. A frustration, but necessary if he is to see out his journey. Fortunately the temperature is a little cooler today and he opens his shirt to the waist, the draft of coastal breezes a boon for the next stage of his route, a twenty-odd-mile trek to the port of Derna, where he means to follow the path of the coastal highway to towns he hopes might still be garrisoned by Allied forces. He will be put to question on his arrival, of course, but he has his story ready, his evidence to hand: that he has broken against all odds from the desert after being left for dead. That he has hiked his way along the edge of the country in a brave effort to rejoin his countrymen. The model, in fact, of soldierly endeavour.

He pauses to take a drink and realises that his canteen is already near empty despite his thrift. Not so worrisome a danger in these fertile shorelands, but even so he will need to ration himself more strictly, be extra vigilant for any chance to resupply. He shouldn't count on anything.

A little farther, and he finds an Italian field cap trodden into the gravel, the discovery surprising him. The owner a refugee like himself, perhaps. There might be a body later on, laid out as a warning, or a makeshift dwelling, the fugitive having instead settled into hermitry. The same fates that Lucchi might have faced had he managed to secure his freedom and flee into the mountains, pausing in that better version of events to study under the moonlight his wedding ring and wristwatch, waiting and watching until finally picking his moment to pass unseen back into the desert, and from there trekking to a highway to thumb a lift from a German keen to buy eggs, or perhaps another collecting ID tags as talismans. His adventure concluding with a report to his wife that he had faced certain death, but had been delivered by a fellow wayfarer with the courage to argue for him. A history that but for a cruel twist of fate might well have played out.

In any case, a kinder revision.

By nightfall the rider comes to the outskirts of Derna, the generality of the town ushered up against its harbour by a steep range of plateaux and gorges. Scrambling up to a vantage point, he sees from a distance German vehicles with blackout headlights travelling its streets and byways. And, on one of the main roads, several groups of soldiers attending a small convoy of supply trucks and wagons. Impossible now to travel across lower ground, the danger of being caught or shot too great. He'll have to make his way over the brow – a far more punishing route – and hope that he can be stealthy enough to pass unnoticed.

The last of his canteen water gone, he takes one of the cactus fruits from his bag and halves it with a knife then squeezes it into his mouth, glad even for so bitter a refreshment. The muscles of his thighs and calves burning, his feet blistered, his shoulders chafed. Even with such a generosity of stops, he has forced himself beyond anything he thought himself capable of, and now there is the price for it. You won't make it, Mawdsley would have told him. Too much to ask of your damaged lungs, your weakened heart. Inconceivable that he might manage the remainder of the journey. And yet if he can just find some resting place for the night, evaluate again in the morning . . .

He heaves his bag onto his shoulders, and begins to clamber over the hillside, slipping and sliding on loose gravel as he tries to keep himself as low as possible. No reason for even goatherds to be up on these empty heights, the Germans likely to presume him an infiltrator and fire upon him without question if he is sighted. A thought which causes him to measure out his progress with caution, scanning every now and then for any signal of alert as he makes his painstaking ascent. At the first summit he is obliged to rest and catch his breath, his hands and knees grazed, the onset of a deep nausea making him worried for a time that the cactus fruit might have been poisonous. But more likely a consequence of circulatory deficiency, the unequal distribution of vital minerals and elements. He could succumb at any time, shrugged from the mountainside to tumble down into the ranks of a bemused enemy, his cause of death mysterious. If only for some damned water!

The sound of an explosion pulls his gaze towards the town, a bright petrol fire sprouting from somewhere close to the harbour. But no sound of aircraft or ships' guns. An accident, then, or some kind of covert action. Whichever, it's his perfect opportunity, any attention now drawn from the hills. He gathers himself up and resumes his progress, determined to make whatever ground he can during the disturbance. But the light is deceptive, the surface of the plateau illuminated in one instant by a tower of flame, the next plunged into darkness, leaving him to hurry unsighted across ground laid with rocks, split by ancient shifts. He can't seem to make a straight line, the balancing canals confused, his legs refusing plain direction.

And then the drop, arrived from nowhere and opening out beneath him as a gulf of unfilled air, into which he tumbles with not so much as a yelp of surprise. He feels his knuckles smash against stone, the kitbag's strap whip across his chin, his flailing body lit for a split second by a fresh column of fire from the harbour. The landing is done with before he even realises it, his arms and legs brought to a crushing stop, the air smacked temporarily from his lungs. The agony holds off for several moments and then rushes over him, the shock of it threatening unconsciousness. What has he done? What idiocy? He tries to move position and immediately stops, the pain forcing a sharp sigh from him. He gingerly turns his head – relieved that he has that much movement – to find himself at the foot of a wide gully, its floor littered with boulders. Not the worst spot, if one were seeking a hiding place. But then if he has sustained serious injury . . .

He tries to unfold himself, nervous of discovering any protruding bones or separated joints. The pain particularly savage in his left knee, which he thinks he must have twisted. He probes the swelling tissue around the joint, wincing at the discomfort, then leans back against the rock face. It will be hard to walk on that leg, let alone haul himself from the bottom of this sheer trap. And so needless! Such careless haste. He drags over his kitbag and pulls out a stale biscuit to eat. He unrolls his blanket and carefully wraps it about himself, unable to keep his eyes from closing as more flames lighten the sky.

18

He wakes in the morning to a pink light flushing the depths of the gulley, and he lies still for a while as sunlight begins to cross his legs. It would be easier if he could just stay here a while and allow himself some rest. But after the disturbances of the previous night, it's possible there'll be search parties. He'll have to do what he can to move on, even in this poor state.

He groans as he pushes himself upright, his limbs stiffened, his fingers and toes numb from the cold, or perhaps from the restriction of blood. He opens his kitbag and rummages inside it for the remaining cactus fruit, finding it crushed in the fall. He breaks apart the skin to squeeze out some moisture. The last of the biscuits now, too, a meagre breakfast to set him on his way. He rolls up his blanket and collects the kitbag and postbag of letters, then tries to stand. His knee the worst, purpled now from the contusion, and grotesquely swollen. Ligament damage, perhaps. If he's lucky, only bruising. Either way, an unpleasant hindrance.

The gulley's walls insurmountable, he decides to track the path of its base, following what he estimates to be a southward course until the channel eventually tapers and breaks into several subsidiaries, each becoming less steep. Trailing his injured leg, he pulls his way up over a slope of scree to find himself overlooking a sweep of blank desert. So he has managed by chance to put the hills between himself and Derna. If he can now make his way down, then he might track the base of the intervening heights until they lead him to the coastal highway. Everything in lesser stages.

He finds it easier to slide down than to climb, lifting his elbows clear as he toboggans short stretches of the descent. A series of low steppes at the hillside's base allowing him finally to limp from one to the next until he reaches level ground. And then there is only the desert to adorn his travel, the heat building as his energy and concentration steadily drain.

It takes several hours of sluggish travel before he arrives within sight of the coastal highway, a pale stripe running proud of the surrounding terrain, no more auspicious in construction than those the deserters had crossed. At first he treks alongside it and at a prudent distance, mindful of the suddenness with which traffic can appear. But thirst and the pain of his injury make any progress a trial, every rock and scrub a wearying obstacle. The highway by comparison a luxury, panacea for a host of discomforts. In this condition, he has little choice.

And from then there is no sound to distract him but the hum of wind, or the grind of his own boots on gravel, the causeway a lustrous marvel laid out before him. He knows that he is dehydrated, his mind in consequence exaggerating nature, but still he finds himself captivated. An empty and cracked tortoiseshell inhabited by a snake. The carcass of a camel, its hide collapsed over exploded ribs, the word 'Jerry' daubed on its flanks. The sand across the road's surface sculpted here and there into perplexing glyphs: a man holding a pistol upon another man. A skull without a jaw.

A check to his rear pulls him to a halt as he sees a spout of dust rising from the needlepoint of the westbound highway. Enemy traffic, almost certainly. He steps from the road onto its sand-drifted verges, and from there shuffles back into the enveloping desert, breathless by the time he reaches the cover of a tall hummock. A supply convoy of four trucks escorted by a command car and two motorcycles venting powder as they trundle past. A resupply to forward lines, perhaps. Brinkhurst may well have been right, any Allied forces now swept ignominiously from the map. An entire coalition of deserters readying to flee the country if he might only summon the strength to join them.

He is still waiting for the road to clear when a collection of white buildings distantly south of his position catches his eye. And even more miraculously, a sleeve of stone risen from the nearby ground. Indistinct in the boil of air, only fleetingly solid. But, a *bir*. Water. It has to be.

When he is certain the last of the traffic has passed, he decides to leave his baggage and carry with him only his canteen as he begins across a field of loose sand and rocks, the underlying crust lifting and diving as though arrested in the action of a wave. The sun is blinding, sweat creeping into his eyes, his breathing as loud to him as slides of shale. He loses his footing and trips, panicking in the moment that he will hit the surface like a thing of glass and break completely. The impact tearing skin from both palms, his injured knee catching a rock, leaving him curled in agony. And still with only a fraction of the distance covered. He sits upright, rocking in pain, staring at his objective with the sudden fear it might dissolve away before him. You need to gather yourself up, find a way forward. Draw your mind away from your body. What will your answers be when they interrogate you, your allies and protectors? What certainties can you offer?

Why no ID, Lieutenant Tuck?

A precaution in the event of capture.

But a precaution against what? What could you know? As a junior officer? Nothing of value, surely.

He heaves himself up, pushes onward.

Divisional strength, battle plans!

The battle was over, the division routed.

I didn't know.

What became of your crew?

The details aren't clear. I'm sure it'll come back to me.

He missteps again, managing this time to stay on his feet.

Do you feel you did anything wrong? Did you make a mistake? Did you let people down?

No need to ask that. It's incriminatory, offensive. I refute the question!

We only want the truth.

It's as I've explained.

Think again.

I did the best I could. It comes down to luck. I brought their letters with me. All of them.

As a penance?

In fellowship.

And these others you ran with. These deserters. You were with them against your will?

Almost there. The buildings are all real, the well real. His boot nudges against a wooden sign lying face down on the sand. He rests on his good knee to lift it. Against my will? Yes, from the very start. He turns the sign over.

Vorsicht!

Typhus

Think again.

He lets the board drop and sits in the dust, bewildered. If he looks into the huts' blank doorways he can see it all now. The ferrying of shrouded corpses, the ever-dwindling cortèges. No graveyard here, all having been slid back into the desert. Swann would approve. He licks his broken lips, stinging them. Why had they taken down the sign? Because the well has been declared safe? He could risk it. Just a small amount to wet his lips. He rocks forward and hangs his head, almost too exhausted to think. He's heard of drinking blood or urine in place of water, a final squalor. He turns again to view the highway, now a slender thread. Bringing himself to his feet will be hard enough, let alone the return crossing. So much easier to haul himself into one of those dilapidated buildings and wait, commit himself in full to the act of desertion.

He heaves himself up into the northward breeze, desperate to be carried, each footfall a tectonic murmur. No one will hear, or care. He sees a kinder Brinkhurst at his side, matching his step, his bullet-holed forehead set in a frown of concern.

Are you quite sure it's even worth it, old man? All this struggle?

I can't stop now.

The ex-captain pauses and removes his cap to bat at flies. Well, we must always presume the best of ourselves, mustn't we. He gives a sly wink then veers off, distracted by a stone's glitter.

The rider sucks in oven air. He drops to his undamaged knee, a quantum of energy preserved in the pause. He's almost made it, almost back to where he started. If only he could hear her say his name. That would be his water.

Little by little, now. On all fours if need be. Pick up the postbag. Just the postbag, nothing else matters. Use whatever power is left to you, carry yourself over to the highway. Sit by the side of the road where you'll be seen. A marker of note even in death. You can do that.

He has the idea that three hours pass before the Germans encounter him. But perhaps twice that number, time now subject to the same doubt as distance. He recognises the fading light, the early stars, the rotating charts from Francis Chichester's *Planisphere*, bought from a Cairo bookshop. When the soldiers finally arrive they step down from a truck the colour of the desert and approach with rifles raised, as though he might be a threat. They search his postbag for weapons and then give him water. One of them lifts him up and tells him in English he is going to be all right, and the rider holds dearly to his hand.

And then he is bundled from the road, as lightly and cleanly as though trafficked by the breeze.

Three

19

'How is it out there?' the dying man asks him. 'Still snowing?'

The rider swats away a fly and puts his eye back to the hole in the wall. 'Couple of feet deep now. Probably be skaters out on the pond soon. Some kids making a snowman. With a fedora and a Tommy gun.'

The dying man grunts and shifts onto his side. 'Little Caesar. I've seen that one. They'd better be quick. I think we've got a thaw coming.'

The rider resumes his sitting position, his back against the wall. 'I shouldn't be surprised.'

The dying man nods towards the rider's postbag. 'You could pick another.'

'Which one?'

'What about the one from the kid to his mother.'

'Hopgood-Banks.'

'Haven't heard that one for a while. Have we?'

The rider takes one of the letters from the bag and tugs it from its envelope.

'Just a minute,' says the dying man. He coughs and rolls onto his back, his gaze fixed on the hut's flat ceiling. 'All right. I'm listening.'

Dearest mother,

This is the most difficult letter one could ever write. But I have had a little time to think about what I should most like to say in the event that . . .

'You can skip the beginning,' the dying man tells him. 'Move to the part with the dog.'

The rider rubs his eyes as he tries to focus. The heat inside the hut is overbearing, the stink of sweat and excrement bringing flies through every hole and crack in the dry mud walls. Most days their guards will empty the waste bucket, but sometimes not, allowing the stench to permeate the crushed straw and sackcloth rags on the floor, any incoming air curdled at once into the same foul state.

. . . it seems odd to think about Beaulieu in all of this, but I often imagine myself on my old walk with him across the fields to the stream. How I'd give him a quick cheer if he would

plunge in to chase a rabbit or squirrel. Sometimes when I'm
listening to R/T static I swear I can hear that same noise of him
in the water. It's quite a comfort to . . .

'I've changed my mind about the breed,' interrupts the dying man. 'Not a setter. Something more exotic. A Weimaraner. Or a Portuguese Pointer.'

The rider folds the letter.

'Wonderful dog, a Weimaraner. A king's dog.' The dying man closes his eyes. 'You'd want to walk one in open country.'

The rider puts the letter back in the postbag. 'Perhaps you should try for more sleep.'

'What about you?'

'Draw a little, I suppose.'

The dying man looks up at the walls, each etched with an assortment of images, the outlines of cottages, lanes and streets scored with a length of straw or a fingernail. One picture depicting a village church, monumental amid a wash of dunes.

'Someone will puzzle you out one day,' he says. 'Just from those drawings. They'll decipher you, like the pharaohs. No need even to sign yourself.'

The dying man's name is Ingram, Leonard Geoffrey, a major with the 3rd King's Dragoon Guards, and formerly the commander of an armoured car. His greater story being that he was brought in dead and came miraculously back to life. Or at least as good as dead when the Germans had passed him into the care of their Berber allies, who had dragged his body – the skin of his thigh and flank puckered with bullet wounds – into the rider's den, to leave him untended. The new arrival exciting the rider to a state of panic. What should I do? How should I look after him? That nagging anxiety over a life put once more into his care.

He had bathed his fevered patient's wounds with what little water his guards had allowed, and had watched over him with a benevolent uselessness, every now and then mopping his brow or gripping his arm in comradeship. Until after several days of impending mortality the major's body had against all expectation reconstituted itself, the bullets oozing back through the skin like any common detritus, his colour and vitality gradually returning. 'Where in God's Hell are we?' had been his first enquiry when he had found his voice. The rider doing his best to explain what he himself found inexplicable: that they had been consigned to some makeshift gaol – no grander than a village storehouse – to be guarded by weather-beaten farmers who would only pause from their goat herding or crop gathering to make sure their captives had not treacherously absconded. And occasionally to dispense bowls of the grain slop that passed for food. 'That's handy then,' the major had announced, with the confidence of a man whose body will spit out bullets like old teeth. 'We'll just walk out of here. Right past them. They won't dare lift a finger.'

And yet they had remained imprisoned, maddeningly coy in their ambitions, both lacking the boldness to push against that single wooden door which has no lock and which might so easily give way if they would only put themselves against it. Perhaps because both had feared their bodies might fail them had they tried, the rider still lamed from his injured knee, the major enduring a state of general frailty. It might at one time have been more a question of strategy: do we make off at night when they're likely to be less alert?/Would they shoot us?/Are there Germans stationed nearby who might respond?/Might we have enough strength to run? They had even considered bribing their captors at one point. But then how does one tempt such austere people?

Any thoughts of escape had finally been given up when the major had suffered a relapse, his body stricken with a fresh bout of sickness, as though the bullets had not left without depositing some slow malignancy. At first nausea, then pallor and renewed fever, followed by intractable lassitude, both men agreeing on a likely cause of sepsis while recognising that any brand of infection might be the culprit. There'll be no stupendous recovery this time, and both know it. The only marvel perhaps being the length of time the major might now eke out.

We need medicine, you stupid bastards! We need help!

But no use the rider screaming and raging, battering at the door. He's done it many times and only once elicited a response, when one of the guards had opened the door and threatened to break a rifle butt across his face. The truth of it being that they are not necessarily expected to live.

Ingram stirs on his pallet of straw. 'What's the weather doing?'

'Raining. Tipping it down. There might be a flood. Wash everything away. The Germans, the wogs, the whole lot.'

The major settles back again. 'Good. Bloody good.'

Sometimes when inventing an outdoors for the major, the rider will draw from that inventory of images and episodes now restored to him, each excerpted from an as yet unfinished whole. A country lane striated with tree shadows, he at the controls of a motorcycle, Nell as pillion, her scarf flashing a brilliant white across his mirrors. A picnic outside a tavern on a canal towpath, long boats bisecting the perfectly reflected archway of a bridge. A terraced house in the same faded brick as its neighbours, its courtyard gated in black iron, its paved pathway leading to a vegetable allotment and Anderson shelter. All of these no less clear or well defined for those dysfunctional pathways in the brain, that unshifting filter of red.

But always alongside them those more disturbing vignettes that will leave him anxious and unsettled, their every visitation attended by the sound of familiar voices raised in panic, each given to the same frantic plea.

Skipper! What now?

And always he wants to answer, to reassure. But he can only ever feel his voice tumbling back down his throat. An awful slide into awareness. He's at the end of his tether, that's the problem. That's what he wants to announce. You can't know exactly where and when it's going to happen – that final draining of fortitude – but the moment is unmistakable.

Skipper! Fuck's sake!

Driver reverse! Sharp right, sharp right!

But not quick enough, the tank becoming for an instant a trembling bottle of sound, its skin vibrating with enough violence to stop a heart. White-hot sparks flinted into each congested chamber.

Then the screams of panic from those below. *Jesus! Shit, shit, shit! Skipper! What now?* Wireless op Hopgood-Banks gazing at him with headset dislodged, his features in a rictus of disbelief.

So this is what it feels like. That moment of abject helplessness, stretched pitilessly out.

The rider longs at times for Brinkhurst's shaving mirror so that he might study himself in this new and reduced state. Fully bearded now, and thinner by far, his features – he assumes – brought to sharper definition. As a creature adapted to darkness he imagines his skin must be returning to its natural colour, his hair likewise. He might – ironically – become entirely himself before passing beyond recognition. Every so often he even has a pang for the attentions of Mawdsley; those cynical evaluations and disingenuous prognoses. *A difficult sort to predict.* Though he might pronounce differently if he were to see the rider in his present state, emaciated and weak, ever more prone to episodes of troubled breathing. *It's the lack of nourishment that will likely finish you.*

But the prospect of fresh fruit or meat seems as distant as any army cookhouse, despite the rich smells that occasionally filter into their corrupted air from outside: aromas of cinnamon, lemon, turmeric, sweetly cooked lamb. Leaves from the Mulukhiyya plant, which Ingram explains is of the mint family. Lamb and mint sauce.

Now and then the rider will have dreams of Swann. The lance corporal assuming an ogreish ferocity in the most vivid of them, in which he will lunge like some cobra-tattooed troll from the granite underpinnings of a bridge, Bren in hand. Each waking leaving the rider freshly persuaded that the truth of a man is quickly outlived by the common interpretation of him. On one occasion he had constructed for himself an entire coda to the lance corporal's story, the episode revisited so many times since – each time with such startling precision – that it would be hard now not to think of the fabrication as history. It will begin when the Italians come to the fallen citadel, determined to revenge themselves for the deserters' raid. The episode at once becoming a bitter contest of attrition as the lance corporal hangs on to his defence, the palace grounds becoming strewn with the bodies of his besiegers. Until at last the engagement will see him retreated into the shelter of the grotto, breathless and bloodied, stubbornly defiant. Fucken bastards, tryin' to move in on my Ritz! Try it now. Just fucken try!

And then that final irony: a scorpion sheltering beneath the kitbags, provoked into a strike by a sudden slide of the lance corporal's ankle. An ending that leaves him sickened with disappointment as he spends his last minutes laid paternally across the Bren, the pathways to his lungs gradually closing. A gross unfairness, perhaps, after so tenacious a display. Yet a conclusion possessing a certain poetry, decides the rider. A tailored justice.

But then in another imagining there is a different fate, which sees the same man in old age, whiling away the hours tending the plots of a modest homestead, his Senussi wife by his side. All alertness gone from him now, any quickness to temper.

The better version of him arrived at only in that second and greater life.

Both the rider and Ingram estimate it to be mid-August, marking the beginning of their second month in captivity together. But it's hard to be certain, their attempts to maintain a calendar long since abandoned. An accurate logging of time would in any case be a route to despondency, and both of them prefer to think of a single day as being of indeterminate length, each man sleeping and waking according to his moods and patterns. A day might only be minutes. Or it might span a week or more. The world might entirely change in a day.

Ingram seems particularly proficient at diverting with stories and anecdotes, having at his command an enviable catalogue of them, and is apt to rouse himself now and then from his ghost-like state to regale the rider with legends of debauchment, ill discipline and other associated misdemeanours. 'Did I tell you about the opium haul they found on the docks at Alex? The poor sod who lost an eye to a green parrot in a Clot Bey brothel? Did you hear about those halfwits who fished a croc out of the Nile at Giza? Of all the hare-brained ideas!'

On his own particular mishap and subsequent capture the major had always been less forthcoming, causing the rider to wonder if he had been another to arrange for himself his own retirement. 'We were in support of the 22nd Armoured,' had been the bones of it, 'and the lot of us took a hellish beating at Knightsbridge. A hit from an AP round killed our driver, and the rest of us couldn't blag a ride. Lasted a good while on foot before we had the idea of trying to make off with a Kraut truck. Bloody stupid idea. Went and got ourselves killed, didn't we. What clowns!'

But the work, nonetheless, of dutiful soldiers, thinks the rider, if one were to accept the story as truth. 'We were attacked by Senussi Arabs,' he had narrated in turn. 'We had an Italian prisoner. The same man whose letter we have. They were determined to hang him, and Corporal Swann and I wouldn't stand for it. They had guns on us from a ridge so we had to find cover behind a few broken walls.'

'Always the same with the wogs,' had said the major. 'Smiling one minute, then a knife between your shoulders the next.'

'We held them off for as long as we could but our ammo was stored in a cave and we couldn't reach it. I was going to make a run for it and hope they wouldn't be quick enough to draw a bead, but one of them managed to put a bullet in our Italian. And that was the end of it.'

'All over an Itie. You might have saved the ammo.'

'He was our prisoner,' the rider had reminded.

Leaving nothing further to add to it.

20

Despite any details of a forgotten life returned to him, the rider finds his best distraction in looking to the future, his fantasy of a journey home now so fully realised that it seems almost a foretelling rather than delusion. His departure from the village eliciting only a bemused apathy from his captors, his travel unimpeded this time by the harshness of the ground, so that he is brought without hindrance across the Akhdar range to overlook that familiar causeway. And how far now? Almost nothing compared to the miles so far covered. Already he finds himself marching the distance, gathering his breath as he walks, any breached lung tissue finally welded over, the blood strengthened. A man of new and stouter heart, bold and ready to flag down British soldiers when next they pass, eager to submit himself.

Where did you come from?

From unscouted desert, and then captivity. A rare tale!

And where are you headed for?

For home and a waiting wife.

To what reward?

To claim everything owed to us.

The fantasy from there leaping on to a rain-lashed village road leading to her house, his motorcycle sheeted over outside it. And once again that knock at her door, bringing her to her step. *I'm sorry to trouble you . . .*

Then afterwards? A rebuilt life, both of them winding back the years. A medical discharge from his regiment, with perhaps a teacher's job to follow. History or music, either would suit. While the factory she works in might return in peace to the manufacture of automobile parts or farm machinery, allowing her to quit her place at the workbench to take up the duties of motherhood. A son, rendered for now in his own likeness, who will one day sit entranced at the feats of his father. An unlikely survival, a desert trek, an escape from captivity, the old injuries carried with pride.

The grand reinvention played out.

'Tell me again how you met her,' says Ingram from his pallet. 'A motorcycle accident, you say?'

'Yes, but the details are still . . .'

'The gist of it, then.'

The rider measures out his words. 'It happened outside her

house. She came out to help. I think it had been raining. The front wheel went away from me in the wet. I trapped my leg under the exhaust. It left a burn just here, on my shin.'

Ingram nods. 'And so she came out. And you saw her standing there, watching, in the rain.' He takes a moment to process the image. 'And what did you say to her?'

'I said, I'm sorry to trouble you. But might you find the time for a rescue?'

Ingram grins. 'So, an opportunistic bastard. Not to mention sly.' His chuckle quickly becoming a splutter and then a series of hacking coughs. 'You could read me your letter,' he says, the rhythm of his breathing restored. 'I know you'd rather not. But I'd be pleased to hear it.'

The rider moves reluctantly to his postbag and draws out a piece of paper, neatly folded. He lifts it into a shaft of light, taking a moment to scan the words. 'It's not necessarily final.'

'Don't worry, I shan't be unkind.'

The rider clears his throat.

Dearest Nell,

I suppose by now you must have received news that I am reported missing. I can't imagine what it must have been like to be told such a thing, and I can only hope that you managed to find the strength to weather it.

I am sure you are reading these words now and thinking that they are not in your husband's hand, and that this must be an

awful mistake. Or worse, some hateful prank. But I can assure
you, my darling . . .

He falters on the open pronouncement of the word.

. . . that as of this date (which I believe to be in the month of
August) I am alive and well and doing everything in my power
to return home. I will not say exactly where I am, but I am
away from battle and in no immediate danger, and my intent
is to remain so until such time as I am able to secure my earliest
passage home.
    As to the reason for my awkward handwriting, I must
confess to an accident some months ago, which caused a little
stiffness in my hand.

He scrutinises the line, suddenly aware of a discrepancy in the
looping of the 'l's and 'f's. His former pencraft returning?

Though you should not worry, as I am recovering well and show
no sign of injury other than a little shortness of breath.

A quick glance towards Ingram, the major raised onto his side,
his face defined in unfleshed bone.

I know this news will upset you, but we must try not to dwell
on such difficulties and think ahead to this second chance.
Although things may at first seem a little strange and different,

you will have a husband again, and I think we can only be
grateful . . .

He glances up to see Ingram's expression, and stops reading.
'You don't approve?'

'I said I shouldn't be unkind.'

The rider folds away his letter, a little embarrassed. 'Sorry to
disappoint. Not lurid enough, perhaps.'

'It's a perfect letter . . . to a stranger. Can you not remember her
at all?'

The rider looks away. 'It's been years.'

'To hell with years. She's your wife.'

'There are pieces missing.'

'Then we'll pick them up for you, shall we? Scrape at the bones
until we get to the meat. And then you can start again. You game
for that?'

He waits for a nod of assent from the rider before relaxing back
into the dark.

Despite the many noises and disturbances admitted through their
thin prison walls, the rider finds that it is those imaginary sounds
which intrude the most. The wail of a sandstorm, the thunder of
distant guns, the sighing of a motorcycle whirling end over end,
locked to the orbit of its own entropic axis. All too easy for him
to pick out the roar of a bow wave, the grind of tracks over gravel,
the swell and wash of fluids gathering in his own chest. And more

troubling still, the intonation of his own confession, the inevitability of which he has become certain, despite his long-held and continuing abstention. Of course he has done his best to prepare for it, but how does one steel oneself against that which festers permanently beneath the skin?

Perhaps after all he had mistaken the nature of his injury. Memories not blown away, as the archdeacon had claimed, but obscured, covered over. That cloud of glass and silt thrown up by a somersaulting motorcycle entered into his head as the medium of disguise. The precious buried alongside the rejected, the dear along with the unconscionable. What's needed is a more clinical approach.

And who better than the major to conduct it? An officer critical of ear and eye, a fellow quick to pass judgement. One might find the very same character on a review board or adjudicating at a court martial. An inquisitor to sit bolt upright and pierce the dark.

Tell me again about the letters, he might begin. How you came by them.

I retrieved them. From a stowage bin. On a burnt-out tank.

Quite a task.

Any of us would have done the same.

And you tore off your insignia because . . .?

Because when I made it back to HQ the entire area had been overrun. Officers were being interrogated.

So you took a despatcher's motorcycle? To make your escape?

Haven't I already told you all this?

No. You haven't told me anything.

May I know the charges against me?

That you could have done more, that you could have pre-vented tragedy.

You want a scapegoat. That's what it is. It's not even fair to ask me this. Look at me. I'm at a low ebb.

One last question: why didn't you take the ring?

The ring?

Your wedding ring. Why didn't you take it? From the locker, where you kept it with the letters. For safe keeping.

You want me to set it all out in detail. Minute by minute, blow by blow. Well, I can't do it. You have to appreciate what it was like. There wasn't the time. I had to leave it. Is there anything else?

Is that your best and fullest account?

Yes. Am I exonerated?

Do you think you should be?

No.

Though the irony is that there had briefly existed a version of him who might have argued otherwise. That same man upon whom had been visited, in a millisecond of explosive detonation, a state of grace. If only he might re-engineer that same release now. An acquittal by mine and bomb.

But he can no longer look to a defence in fugue, the weight of recovered detail speaking too loud against him. That second lieu-tenant who had written his final letter of devotion being the same man who must now assume the burden of shame.

And if at last he should make his return to her, would she even understand it? That the reliving of a single day should rule every day to come? But there was nothing you could have done differently, she might say to him. You couldn't have changed the outcome. This in the assumption that some blame might be argued away. That those protective fictions, once so artfully built, might somehow be restored. The only consequence to such ministrations being a cruel reopening of the wound.

Gunner, targets now at two-zero-zero-zero. AP rounds on my go, take your pick.

All these men in his care. His fellow commanders poised in their turrets, field glasses to their eyes, each of them trusting that their squadron leader will stay calm, stay clear-headed, that he will see a way through. As though any man here could be so blanketed from fear. The very bedrock beneath them humming to the boom of their tanks' aero engines. Every fabric and metal becoming acrid in the heat.

Fire!

Even now it stays with him: that wave of shock upon recoil, the entire body of the vehicle in spasm. Inkblots at once staining the sky above the forces set against them.

Driver advance! Flat out, flat out!

And then the rush to movement, allowing a release of sorts, a recourse to that which has become automatic, mechanical in nature. His switching of the wireless control between VHF and intercom performed with machinelike precision. His regular clicking of the microphone switch lending a beat to the chaos.

George 1. Get your arses away from that ridge! Head for the next and keep firing. Off. Who's that stuck over there? Get moving for Christ's sake. Off.

Until that most dread of alerts, bursting sharply through the headset chatter and white noise. *Eighty-eight crews flanking left.*

Eighty-eight: so innocuous a term for so malevolent a weapon, the huge anti-aircraft guns able to crumple a tank like tinfoil from as great a distance as a mile and a half.

George 1. Eighty-eights reported. Watch your broadsides everyone. Keep moving. Off.

But already too late for one crew, the steel walls of their Grant suddenly collapsed, the explosion of on-board ammunition sending escape hatches and viewport shields spinning from the carcass. And then another claimed straight afterwards, its turret blasted upward like a kettle lid to land upturned in the dust.

And the same fate, no doubt, for all. Any moment now. Any second. His weakening thighs and knees braced against turret walls, clouds of oil smoke obscuring any periscope view, palls of cordite stinging at his eyes. Any vestiges of resolve cancelled at once by the shell that whines overhead to burst only yards behind, spraying the hull with shrapnel.

Jesus!/Shit, shit, shit!/Everybody all right?/We're OK, we're OK.

No damage to the running gear, mercifully. But the antenna is gone, no further instruction to the squadron possible.

Skipper! What now?

He ought to lead them forward. That would be the better tactic. Not to allow the eighty-eight crews to pick out targets. But to embark upon that murdering ground ...

He shouldn't abandon the squadron. He knows he shouldn't. But then perhaps the others might spot his manoeuvre and do likewise.

Driver reverse. Sharp right, sharp right!

And already the guilt is there. That he is withdrawing a serviceable vehicle from the field. That he is doing so without regard for all those under his command. A shame that cuts even deeper as he puts his eyes back to the periscope to see another of the squadron's tanks wheeling violently apart.

And yet still it's not enough. He has to be out of it, this stifling cell. He needs unconfined space, smokeless air. That shallow ridge ahead will do. He simply can't wait any longer.

Driver halt! Halt, goddamn it! Can't see a thing, I need to take a look.

But no one among his crew will copy his escape, because he is their commander and he has their trust. A reconnaissance, he had said. An absolute betrayal when he has no such intention, his only impulse being to settle himself into sheltering thoughts. The warmth of her gathered to him in the dark, the thrill of her breath across the back of his neck, the tentativeness of her touch against his cheek. The entire language of her given over to that single imploration for his return.

And then the impact, throwing him onto his back, clapping the breath from him. The flush of searing heat across his cheeks and forearms signalling the worst before he even sees it. The Grant gutshot and killed, its flanks already choked in yellow fire.

Bail out. Bail out now.

Please God.

No one emerging. No hatch opening. His terrible and undisputed handiwork.

Under poetic law there would be a summary justice for it; an airstrike, a providential shell, some means by which he might be obliterated. But instead he knows there will be hearings and testimonies, the complete, inglorious portrait of him held up for all to see. Better to acknowledge the crime now, to throw off those emblems and insignia of which he has proved so unworthy and submit himself to the desert, to its shrouding dust and purgative winds.

And of those collected farewells, secure in their protective locker: he will recover them if he can, his wardship of them intended not only as a contrition but an act of faith. That we endure in the words we have written and thoughts we have laid out, each of us unimpeachable in that better version of ourselves.

Why didn't you take the ring? she will ask.

Because that man didn't deserve it. That man who had a home and a wife.

She will nod, heartbroken. And there's nothing else you have for me?

No, I think not. I think at last we have the final story of me.

21

The major's time is up. It's apparent to the rider even if not to Ingram himself, his advancing delirium perhaps shielding him from any deeper awareness. Over the past few days he has declined beyond any recovery, the skin purpling beneath his sunken eyes, his teeth stained from weeping gums. Most of his remaining hours spent asleep except for those moments he will awake to stare into space, an emaciated watchman, his attention commanded by something deeper in the gloom. There's little to be done now except to watch and wait, and hope for the gentlest end.

He begins his last day with a series of loud moans, rousing the rider from his sleep. No attempts at language but simply reflexive outbursts. Even so, the rider makes his best attempt to comfort, placing a calming hand on his shoulder while offering quiet encouragements. Best to sleep now. It won't help to be awake. His efforts rewarded only with the occasional anguished outcry. 'Why are you here?' And, 'What are you trying to steal from me?'

Then the major's attention will drift, allowing the rider to withdraw, wary of further bouts of madness. It's in his mind to call for the guards and point out that his cellmate is already a dead man, have them remove him in advance. But guilt annuls the idea, leaving him to sit in silence and watch as the major will every so often raise up his hands to perform a slow ballet, as though to finesse himself through these final hours.

When at last he lapses back into unconsciousness the rider gratefully reclines, hoping on his next waking to find the whole business discreetly concluded. But the dying man will not slip off so easily, a weary summons from him again breaking the stillness, once more obliging the rider to attend him.

'You have to get back. Make something, build something. It's on you, the ones who go home. Don't you dare squander it. Don't you bloody dare.'

His last decree before the work of dying. A task the rider abandons him to while observing from a respectful distance. What else should he do? There are no palliatives, and the burden can't be shared. It's a perdition for both, in truth, the major's protracted surrender both wearying and saddening to witness. By early afternoon his body appears in the grip of an inescapable torpor, only his eyes showing any vestiges of animation before they too paralyse, his gaze settled on something beyond the prison walls. Once the rider is certain the process is finished he tentatively feels for a pulse, then goes to the door to begin beating on it with his fist. There's a man dead in here! Do you hear me? You need to take him away! You need to bury him!

They don't come, of course, one alarm as spurious as the next. There are crops to be tended, goats to milk, the order of the day already set. The rider gives up at last, and covers over the major's face with straw while he waits for the usual ration of stale bread and grain porridge to be delivered.

Not until he wakes from a period of slumber in late afternoon does he find the body at last taken, removed no doubt into some unmarked pit from where it will never be recovered. The tale of Major Leonard Geoffrey Ingram to become as dubious as any campfire yarn.

Time slows after the major's passing. It's to be expected, with no banter or repartee to fill the hours and days. No new experiences for the rider to gather, nothing to be learnt or assimilated. Instead he is compelled to become of deeper interest to himself. The flesh is withering, perhaps even the bones reducing as in old age; things which ought certainly to be logged. And so he notes on the walls the measurements he takes of himself, building up the dimensional record. The thighbone two palms in girth, the anklebones but one. An eye orbit documented in the fleshy base of a thumb. If he places both hands about his hips then they will fail to meet only by the length of a ring finger, a distance under imminent threat of collapse. And it will continue, this diminution, until he is entirely reshaped. But into who? Witnesses would be useful. Someone with a camera.

And then something quite remarkable. They leave the door open! On a morning otherwise quite ordinary. And not by mistake either, the gap too inviting. A trap, then. He is meant to attempt an escape, handing them a reason to gun him down, ending their responsibility for him. Well he won't fall for it!

He sits for a time and waits, his eyes adjusting to the pyramid of brilliance across the floor. Until it occurs to him that his captors have little need of subterfuge if they mean to finish him. Simple enough for them to commit straightforward murder and fabricate the circumstance later. Perhaps it's not as it seems.

He eases the door further open to look out upon a scene of surprising calm, a sparse collection of clay dwellings accompanied by several small livestock pens and a modest stable. There are goatskins hung to dry, cloths of different hues stretched from a wooden frame. An old man blithely regarding him from amid a throng of terracotta jugs, a pregnant woman sparing him a nervous glance in passing. He can hear someone humming, a blade being sharpened. In the gaps between buildings he spies the bright red of the ocean, and it takes the breath from him. That he should have allowed himself to be held here so long, starving and subdued, without ever daring to test his confinement. That he and the major had never inspired one another to greater courage.

He is about to wander further from the gaolhouse when one

of the guards scurries around the side of the building and blocks his path, at once berating him while raising the barrel of an antique rifle to his face, the odours of stale gunpowder and goat grease wafted under his nose until he is forced back to the door-way of the prison, where he folds like a pack of cards on his own joints. The Berber finishing with a high-pitched tirade before withdrawing a little way to watch, wary that the escapee might spring up to resume his flight.

The rider shades his eyes, confused in the sun's heat. His tor-mentor rested now against a wooden post, from where he idly spits tobacco juice onto the sand.

A thoroughly rude chap, no doubt.

Brinkhurst might have approved the epithet.

He thinks it is because the Germans have left that he is allowed this extra freedom. If not formally or officially left, then at least maintaining a conspicuous absence. And presumably without leaving any instructions for his transportation or disposal. Perhaps there's more to it still, rumours continually drifting in to settle about the ears of any disposed to receive them. It's all finished! The war is done with, the Axis powers abandoning the desert! All of it communicated to the rider in a code of furtive glances, the occasional and inadvertent relay of surprise. But the British were beaten . . . quite defeated . . . How does such a thing happen?

Generally it will be Rude Chap or one of the other regular

guards – rechristened in these more cordial times as Dour Chap, Fierce Chap and Happy Chap – who will fetch him his bowls of food and fresh water. A chair fashioned from an old saddle and footstool now set out for him as his fool's throne so that he can spend his afternoons stretched out to dry. He is given a fixed perimeter within which to exercise, his feet collecting dirt like flaccid shovelheads. Except that no one seems quite certain on the boundary, provoking regular argument over the matter, Happy Chap becoming markedly more fierce than Fierce Chap, who will invariably retreat into the most intractable dourness. Each in the end cancelling out one another's tempers.

The rider wonders if he might not just walk away. Leave them to their tiresome squabbles and discreetly abscond. But with what consequences? He's clearly supposed to wait. If not for the Germans, then for the British. His captors perhaps envisaging some formal exchange, a handing over from which they will depart recompensed. If there was any way to barter his way free ...

But then perhaps there's some advantage in this prolonged isolation. There are preparations to be made, things to be settled upon, if he is ever to re-enter the wider world. And foremost among them, the story of his adventure. If it should ever come to the point of cross-examination, he will need to be beyond doubt, his testimony unimpeachable. He will need to report with authority how he and his fellow soldiers had trekked bravely northward in search of Allied forces, taking casualties along the way. How he and Major Ingram had been separately taken prisoner while attempting to rejoin their own lines, the major succumbing at last to his wounds.

And most importantly of all, how he had come – despite every care and diligence – so tragically to lose his crew. The precise circumstances of it, the exact sequence of disaster as he can best recall it. There'll be some leeway here, of course, given the fog of war. Things will happen so quickly in the melee of battle that it's not always possible to register events with any certainty. The mind sometimes making exclusions from the record. That filter engaged not as a mercy but as a survival instinct.

22

The rider learns that there is to be a renovation of his former gaol cell, and now lowly garret. Though the intent is not immediately apparent when a train of womenfolk enter one afternoon to sweep and mop the floors, any old or polluted bedding transported away with them. An eviction, perhaps? But then they return with fresh bedding and a scattering of furniture in the way of stools, a table and a small brass French paraffin stove – *Garanti Inexplosible* – which they set down with a ritual deliberation in the centre of the room. And then a jar of fluid, which he takes to be alcohol, handed to him by a veiled crone with seared-off fingertips, the bestowal made with an extravagant gesture of warning. *Mind yourself. With this you could destroy everything!*

And still his assimilation into village life continues, those

months of incarceration becoming with distance more probationary than malign. They begin to entrust him with menial
tasks, each to be conducted according to the robustness of his
constitution. The scraping of skins, the collecting of earthenware,
the tending of a goat, the plucking of a chicken – that duty awak-
ing in him a particular disquiet. After hearing him coughing one
morning they even arrange for him a doctor's visit, the fellow in
question arriving with his tonics and victuals in a briefcase of
Italian leather fastened with gold-plated clasps, like a man from
the ministry come to take the minutes of his condition. A hearty
massage of his chest and a lengthy monitoring of his breathing
leading the official to conclude ... what? His pronouncements
eliciting a black-toothed grin from Happy Chap. An endorse-
ment for his carers then, at least. A paragon of healing!

And thereafter a greater transformation still, his soldier's garments at last taken from him and burnt, fresh robes bestowed to
him before he is led like an apostle to a small olive grove to spend
the hours collecting fruit into a basket while meditating on the
nature of his ordainment. This simpler and more pious life. And
his final permission to withdraw.

He wakes one morning to the sound of rain, the rattle of drops
across the prison roof pulling him in curiosity to the doorway.
Almost unreal to see the village awash, its hard earth now slicked
and rutted, an alarmed mule mired at its tether, every hollow
vessel in sight turned upward for collection. The skies, he thinks,

almost English. And perhaps it's that pang of nostalgia – some barely understood yearning – that decides it for him. He can't be here any longer.

But how to announce it, there's the difficulty. How to break it to his genial captors? Why leave, after all, when he has become so settled? And of course he can't explain it to them, can't sketch or draw the reasons in any way they might understand. It'll feel like a betrayal, inevitably. After all they've done for him. It'll feel like a desertion.

From the cover of his den he spies Fierce Chap striding towards an animal pen, a young goat in his arms. Perhaps the ideal fellow with whom to broach the matter. A man whose general disdain might dispose him towards granting a release.

He weighs the opportunity for as long as he dares, then snatches up a blanket and holds it over his head as he slips out into the downpour, stepping carefully across runnels and streamlets until he arrives within yards of the Berber, the blanket over his head already sodden.

'I'm leaving,' he says. 'I'm going that way.' He points eastward along the coast. 'To the British road.'

The Berber sets down the kid in the corral and returns his unblinking attention to the rider.

'Do you understand what I'm saying? It's time for me to go. I can't stay here. I'm going back. Today.'

Is that it? Is it done? It's hard to tell, Fierce Chap's expression remaining quite unreadable. Which one could take as either assent or disapproval. Or simply a lack of comprehension.

Though at least when the rider turns away from him to head back to the grain store, there are no threats to follow him, nor any promise of retribution should he try such a thing. Simply the same inscrutable silence. But perhaps the Berber is already planning how to pass on the news to his compatriots, while adding his own particular counsel: that to let their prisoner go would be the wisest choice, given the tides of war. Or that they should simply attribute his leaving to the same supernaturalism that brought the entire day. The rains came, and the Englishman left. People must make of it what they will.

They provision him as best they can for his journey, supplying him with bread, chickpea cakes, strips of dried meat and a handful of dates. They fill a water skin for him and help heave it over his shoulder. One of the women bestows a blessing upon him, though in performance it seems more an admonishment. *May God bring you to your deserved path.*

Fierce Chap is elected to be his guide for the first part of his travel, chagrined though he appears to be at the inconvenience, and a small group gathers to see him off, Happy Chap, Rude Chap and Dour Chap among them. He's not quite sure how to say his goodbye to them, no one stepping forward to offer their hand or submit themselves to an embrace. Certainly the most inert of farewells. He decides in the end to offer a salute, which he realises must look absurd even as he executes it, his fingertips snapping smartly to the cloth of his headdress. The instinct of an officer, despite all. Though he imagines they must all recognise the charade.

When the ceremony is concluded, Fierce Chap leads him from the perimeter of the village, their route taking them beyond sight of the settlement and across a dishevelled coastal plain, its thin topsoil rinsed from a jumble of stone crests like the rudders and sternposts to a capsized fleet. And then through a wide, tree-lined cleft in the ground, rainfall cascading through the higher branches. The Berber all the while walking on ahead, occasionally casting a backward glance to make sure of his charge. His shoulders invariably drooping whenever he sees the rider pause to collect his breath. Are all foreigners so exhausted by war?

As they begin their ascent to higher ground the rain at last abates, though the soil remains by turn slippery and cloying, every steppe and platform treacherously greased. And if the rider had believed himself capable of the efforts required, then the doubts are quick to return. Those butterfly lungs, a straining heart, the consequences of altered air pressure and extreme humidity. Already from the corner of his eye he can see Fierce Chap looking to him with concern, as though he might be witnessing the slow collapse of a building or the opening of a great chasm.

He sits heavily and stretches out his fingers, finding a stream of collected water. The beginnings of a great flood, if there were any God at all. An Old Testament cleansing, every soldier and combatant sluiced from their trenches and leaguers out into the ocean. A grand release for all.

And perhaps only with such a cleansing could the most

infamous of acts be expunged. The betrayal of one's comrades, the
abandonment of a wife, the murder of a prisoner of war, all those
charges already entered into the record as rumours and echoes,
inimical to his every future. And, most damning of all, the spec-
tre of that minutes-long wait during which he will look to the
open turret of a tank, knowing at the same time that all inside
will be fumbling in that cramped and smoke-filled cell to unhook
themselves from belts, wires and hoses, each of them squeezing
themselves up against scalding metal to try and push their way
out, their lungs filling with poisons, their skins beginning to
shrink and blister. Hoppy, Oxo, Jack, Lindo, Fitz.

What can he do?

Leant upon the shoulder of his guide, the rider recommits himself to the remainder of the ascent, both men at last arriving upon
a plateau described in fieldworks and acres of tilled earth, where
the Berber is able to point out the familiar interval of blankness
that lies south of the mountains. And through it the pale track of
the coastal highway, picked out now by sunlight.

Sensing that this will be their moment of parting, the rider
takes himself aside and pulls from his postbag both of the letters
written to her – one from the turret of a tank, the other from the
squalor of a prison cell. As if there might ever have been a choice
between them.

You will be brave again when I am gone.

He places the first letter back into the postbag, crumpling the second into his pocket. He turns back to Fierce Chap and extends to him the bag. 'Please take these. For when the British come.'

The Berber continues to view him with some suspicion, unsure whether to receive the bequeathal as gift or liability.

'In case you were wondering . . .' says the rider. 'My name was Second Lieutenant James Tuck of the Third Tank Regiment, 7th Armoured Division, His Majesty's Middle Eastern Forces.'

His confession received with a correct and proper silence.

There ought in the end to be some gesture of gratitude, he thinks. At least an acknowledgement of companionship. But before he can arrive at any appropriate means to deliver either, the Berber has already turned to begin his journey home. The rider watches him go, at once moved to a sense of loss. But then what should he have expected? They were never friends.

For a while he sits to observe the distant road, busied now and then by passing traffic. Soldiers on their way home. Or perhaps resigned to their next engagement. It's all beyond him now.

Though if he stares long enough, he can see past the highway into a greater expanse, where that temple of previous imaginings still awaits. No longer some fabulous basilica but a smaller and more austere building, steepled in grey stone. And within its doors an oak-panelled annexe, then a corridor leading to a high-ceilinged chamber, quite empty except for a single desk. The length of the room lit gloomily by a clerestory of arched windows, the wind every now and then bringing seeds against the glass in a steady *tap-tap-tap*. Just like the impact of small-arms fire against steel plate. Exactly that sound.

And if he will look closer still, a scattering of papers on that lone desk, each inscribed with the beginnings of a great work:

Dear Mrs Hopgood-Banks,
Mr and Mrs Oxburgh,
Mr and Mrs Warren,
Mrs Lindqvist,
Mr and Mrs Fitzhugh,
Signora Lucchi,

    I'm writing to let you know that I knew your husband. Your son.
    And that they – to their dire misfortune – knew me.

In the next life, he decides, I shall become everything expected of me.

He picks himself up, using scrub as handholds to secure himself, and begins his renewed ascent towards that high boundary between land and sea, the sun once more strong against his back. A pilgrimage that sees him trek on into his own shadow until it becomes broken over scree and sedge, diffuse beneath a lace of branches. The shape of him given up at length into the sheltering vaultworks of a gorge, its base piped with a congruency of currents and breezes, each met and resolved as though by agency of some perfect and unfailing lung.

Acknowledgements

I would like to thank all the team at Granta, particularly my editor Max Porter for his astuteness and enthusiasm in steering the book towards its final version. Sincere thanks also to my agent Karolina Sutton for ensuring the novel passed into such good hands.

A special thank-you to historian David Fletcher, who was kind enough to guide me around an M3 Grant, and for his insight and expertise on the subject of tank warfare. (Any errors in the text are certainly mine rather than his.) I am grateful to John Lamb for his assistance with the German, and to Gaetano D'Angelo for his help with the Italian. My thanks too to all those who gave moral and material support along the way, including Celia Brayfield, Fay Weldon, Philip Gwyn Jones, Karin Lowachee, Chris Johnson, Henry and Frances Parlour, Philippa Maffioli, and Pat and Malcolm Hobson.

I am indebted also to the authors and editors of the following books, all of which were valuable in providing inspiration and detail for the rider's journey: *Alamein to Zem Zem* by Keith Douglas, *Prisoner from Alamein* by Brian Stone, *A Tankie's Travels* by Jock Watt, *It is Bliss Here* by Myles Hildyard, *Last Letters Home* edited by Tamasin Day-Lewis, *The Desert War Trilogy* by Alan Moorehead, and *Tank Men* by Robert Kershaw.

And finally I must express my deepest thanks and appreciation to Selma Parlour, for her dependably incisive readings and for her patience and encouragement throughout.